Other Books by William Sleator

ODDBALLS

oddballs

stories by

WILLIAM
SLEATOR

Dutton Children's Books

N E W   Y O R K

All of the characters in this book—except for my own family—are fictitious, and any resemblance to actual persons is coincidental.

Library of Congress Cataloging-in-Publication Data

Sleator, William.
Oddballs: stories / by William Sleator.—1st ed.
p. cm.
Summary: A collection of stories based on experiences from the author's youth and peopled with an unusual assortment of family and friends.
ISBN 0-525-45057-2
1. Sleator, William—Juvenile fiction.
[1. Sleator, William—Fiction.   2. Family life—Fiction.
3. Friendship—Fiction.]
I. Title.
PZ7.S63130d   1993
[Fic]—dc20   92-27666   CIP   AC

Published in the United States by Dutton Children's Books, a division of Penguin Books USA Inc.
375 Hudson Street, New York, New York 10014

Editor: Ann Durell   Designer: Sara Reynolds
Printed in U.S.A.
First Edition
10 9 8 7 6 5 4

To my family: Please forgive me!

Contents

ODDBALLS

Games

The best presents our parents ever gave to my sister, Vicky, and me were our little brothers.

I was nine and Vicky was seven and a half when Danny was born. We had been looking forward impatiently to his arrival, especially Vicky, who loved playing with dolls. She had always enjoyed making the dolls fight with each other; when the dolls wore out, she ripped off their arms and legs. Now she is a nurse.

We tried to be more careful with Danny. But it didn't take us long to discover that a human baby with a brain was a lot more fun to play with than a stupid doll.

Before Danny came along, Vicky and I had invented a wonderful game to play on car trips. We pretended we

3

were BMs. We'd wrap ourselves up in an old brown blanket in the back of the station wagon and tell each other our life stories as excrement.

This game had begun on a trip to Canada in 1952, when everybody was celebrating the coronation of Queen Elizabeth. Like most little girls, Vicky idolized the young queen. And so, in the BM game, she usually began her existence as an Oreo cookie or a Hostess cupcake, eaten by Queen Elizabeth at a royal banquet in Buckingham Palace. Vicky always claimed to remember exactly what it had been like in our mother's womb, and she was equally vivid about her metamorphosis from cupcake to BM inside the queen's glamorous intestinal tract. Vicky also described in detail the marble palace bathroom, bigger than our living room at home, and said that being flushed down the queen's toilet was *utterly* more fun than riding the Tilt-a-Whirl.

My adventures were less ritzy. I had been sick from overindulgence two times in my life: Once I had eaten several pints of freshly picked blackberries at our grandmother's house; another time I had devoured too much tzimmes, a Jewish meat-and-carrot stew that was a specialty of our aunt Miriam. My stories tended to begin with these two items, eaten at the same time, making me a purple-and-orange-striped BM. "That's not fair!" Vicky would scream. "BMs aren't striped!" And I would point out that just because *she* had never seen a striped one didn't mean they didn't exist.

But once Danny was born, and Vicky and I were often required to change his diapers, the subject of BMs lost a lot of its charm. We needed a new way to amuse ourselves in the car. And there was Danny. The game we came up with we called Babaloo Bum.

It started on a trip out West when Danny was about six months old. We were in the back of the station wagon with Danny and all the boxes and suitcases, traveling on a bumpy road. Danny loved to be bounced and rocked, which got tiring after awhile. It occurred to us to let the car do this for us. We put him on top of a suitcase. His shifting weight, combined with the bouncing of the car, made the suitcase rock back and forth. But we didn't try to steady it. Danny was enjoying himself; he had no idea that anything might go wrong. It was a total surprise to him when the suitcase tipped over and slammed him onto the floor. He howled.

Chuckling, we set the suitcase on end to make it a little more unstable, balanced a smaller suitcase on top of it, and perched Danny on that. Danny immediately stopped crying and began to smile adorably, comforted by being rocked. The suitcases toppled; Danny hit the floor again and wailed. We shrieked with laughter. Mom and Dad, knowing we would *never* hurt Danny, were amused by our merriment.

The next time we set him up there, we chanted "Babaloo Bum! Babaloo Bum!" He clapped his hands and beamed at us, still oblivious to his danger. Soon our stomachs were sore from laughing. Amazingly, Danny didn't catch on for a long time, and the game entertained us for most of the trip. In fact, it's the only thing I remember about it.

When Danny was about fifteen months old, Mom got pregnant again. We tried to explain to him what was going to happen. We would show him a picture of a baby in a magazine and say, "See this cute, adorable baby, Danny? Aren't we lucky because soon we're going to have a cute, adorable baby in our family, too." We knew he understood when he tore the picture out of the magazine, flung it to the floor, and screamed, "No baby!"

The new baby was *not* as cute as Danny. His head was too big; he looked bald because his hair was so blond; he had a disproportionately large mouth and ears that stuck out. Whenever Aunt Ronnie saw him, she would remark, with a self-satisfied cackle, "He looks just like Uncle Arnold." Uncle Arnold was a mental incompetent who had spent most of his life in institutions.

But Aunt Ronnie's opinion was not a serious problem for the baby. Danny was. From Danny's point of view, the baby was a usurper who had taken too much attention away from him. The baby, who had a sweet and gentle nature, adored his older brother. Danny accepted this affection on good days, helping him build things with blocks and other toys. On bad days, he slapped him around.

Then there was the problem of the new baby's name. As our parents had decided not to have any more kids, this was their last opportunity to name a human being, and they wanted to make a truly creative statement. They came up with lots of interesting names—so many that they couldn't decide which one they preferred. There were also several relatives they felt it would be nice to commemorate by naming this kid after them, but how could they name him after one and not the others?

So they didn't name him anything. Our father referred to him as "that other kid." Vicky and I called him the new baby, which soon evolved into "Newby." And for the first years of his life, while our parents continued to put off the decision, Newby was his name.

When Newby was about two, even Dad, who tended to procrastinate, realized they had to do something about his name. But they still couldn't decide. The only solution was to name him *everything*. And so in the end, the name they put on his birth certificate was Tycho Barney George Clement Newby Sleator.

Now that his official, legal first name was Tycho, Mom and Dad decreed that we should all start calling him that. And so Newby became Tycho. It wasn't easy to remember at first, but Vicky and I liked the novelty of this game and persisted until it became natural to us. The only person in the family who did not enjoy the situation was, of course, Newby, who refused to answer to Tycho for weeks, pouting and looking the other way whenever we said it. We thought this response was very funny.

Having an often abusive older brother, and the fact that everybody in the family started calling him by a completely different name when he was two, were probably the seeds that resulted in Tycho's first great act of independence: He refused to be toilet trained. It was a brilliantly simple and effective method of asserting his control; in spite of being the youngest, he was able to put us all at his mercy. His third birthday came and went, and then his fourth. He was still wearing diapers.

Our parents didn't worry about this. But Vicky and I had to change him a lot. "Tycho, will you *please* do it on the toilet," we would beg him as we cleaned him in the bathtub.

"When I've five," he would obstinately insist.

"Big boys don't do this, Tycho, only disgusting little *babies*," I told him.

"No one will want to play with you if you have smelly BMs in your pants," Vicky added, dumping bubble bath into the tub. "The other kids will hate you and make fun of you."

"Four-year-olds who go in their pants get a horrible

disease and *die*, Tycho; it says so in Mom's medical books."

"Please just do it on the toilet, and we'll give you all the candy you can eat for the rest of your *life*."

He remained steadfast, unyielding, true to his principles. "When I've five" was his constant refrain.

As Tycho's fifth birthday approached, our relief was tinged with uncertainty. It would be wonderful if he kept his promise, but what if he didn't? Would he be able to go to school? Would he ever have a girl friend? Would we spend the rest of our lives changing him?

On his fifth birthday, Tycho very calmly and skillfully went on the toilet, as though he'd always done it that way. He's been using the toilet ever since.

Without Tycho's messes to clean up, car trips became a lot pleasanter. By this time, Danny and Tycho were both too old for Babaloo Bum, so we made up more sophisticated games to play with them in the car. In one game, Vicky and I would ask Danny and Tycho to choose which one of us they liked better. They greeted this question with groans, but they were trapped in the car and couldn't get away from us. "If you choose me, I'll give you my dessert tonight—and if you choose Billy, I'll throw you out the window," Vicky would coolly inform Tycho. At first he believed her and would burst into tears. But this game didn't last very long. The marvelous rewards and terrible retribution each of us promised for being chosen or not were never carried out, and Danny and Tycho grew bored. Since the game no longer had an emotional effect on them, it had lost its appeal.

The best car game was called What Would Be Worse? At first it was pretty easy; we would merely ask them to choose between two fates. Even Tycho had no problem coming up with the answer to "Would you rather inherit a huge mansion and be insanely rich for the rest of your life or die without any money at all in a sewer among rats?"

But questions like that weren't much of a challenge, so we quickly began making them more difficult. "What would be worse?" we asked. "To be impaled on a bed of nails and take three days to die or to have all your arms and legs cut off and live?" Or "What would be worse? To spend the rest of your life in jail for a crime you didn't commit or for everyone else in the world to die except you?" Danny and Tycho would become quite bothered by these questions, brooding and sighing gloomily over them for miles, while Vicky and I tried to suppress our chuckles.

Baby-sitting was another good opportunity for games with our little brothers. As adolescents, Vicky and I enjoyed having the run of the house without parental supervision. But Danny and Tycho would sometimes get worried when Mom and Dad went out at night. We got so tired of answering their repeated questions about where Mommy and Daddy were, and when they were coming home, that we were inspired to invent a new game.

"Would you like to hear a little song?" we would ask them. They nodded innocently. We'd go to the piano; I'd play a mournful and heartrending tune, and Vicky would sing:

> *Once there were two little boys,*
> *And one night their mommy*
> *And daddy went out.*
> *They kissed the little boys good-bye*
> *And drove away in the car. . . .*

Now I added melodramatic tremolo, like the music in old-time movies. Danny and Tycho began to sniffle. Vicky's voice grew gentler:

> *And their mommy and daddy*
> *Never came home again.*
> *The little boys cried and cried,*
> *But nobody ever came.*
> *Nobody came to say good-night;*
> *Nobody came to give them their bottles.*
> *They never saw their mommy and daddy again.*

By this time, Danny and Tycho would be sobbing un-controllably, tears rolling down their cheeks. Even after they knew the song by heart, it still invariably made them cry. And when it was over, they'd always wipe their eyes and beg us, "Play it again. *Please* play it again!"

Baby-sitting was also our chance to teach them every obscene word we knew. Our parents were not upset when Danny and Tycho repeated these words to them. But Danny and Tycho also taught these words to their friends in the neighborhood, and *their* parents were not charmed when they heard their toddlers cursing like teenage gang members. Still, Vicky and I persisted. We spent hours and hours coaching Danny to memorize all the verses of a song called "Canal Street," which was full of nasty words and lewd situations.

Then our grandmother came to visit. Grandma and I were playing Scrabble, pondering silently over the board, when Danny strolled into the room. In his sweet, child-ish, soprano voice, he began to sing. "Walking down Canal Street, knocking on every door—"

"Wait, Danny!" I said, horrified. "Don't bother us now. We're concentrating."

"But I'd love to hear his little song," Grandma said. "Go on, Danny."

And so he sang "Canal Street," one verse after another, not forgetting a single gross syllable. Grandma and I sat there, our eyes on the Scrabble board, until finally Danny wandered away.

Something had to be done. But we couldn't just tell Danny and Tycho never to say those words; that would only guarantee that they'd use them at every possible opportunity. So we took the opposite tack. We invented the word *drang*.

"All those other words we taught you, it doesn't matter if you say them," we told Danny and Tycho. "Just go around and say them to everybody."

"You mean that?" Danny said, narrowing his eyes.

"Sure." Vicky shrugged nonchalantly.

"I mean, at least they're not saying"—my voice dropped—"that other word."

"What other word?" Danny wanted to know.

Vicky and I looked at each other. I started to speak. "No, don't tell them!" Vicky said quickly.

"Tell us!" Danny insisted.

We pressed our lips together and shook our heads.

"If you don't, we'll tell Mommy and Daddy what you and your friends did the other night when they went out and you thought we were asleep," Danny threatened. "Won't we, Tycho?"

Tycho nodded obediently.

"You wouldn't!" Vicky snapped at them, though of course she knew Danny would.

"Maybe we better tell them," I said grimly.

Vicky sighed. She looked around the room to be sure no one else was there. "The other word is . . . *drang*," she reluctantly whispered.

"It's the worst word in the world," I added.

Danny's eyes lit up. "Drang?" he said experimentally, testing the sound on his tongue.

Vicky and I shuddered and closed our eyes. "Don't! If anybody ever hears you say that, they will never forgive you, and they'll hate us because they'll know we taught it to you."

For about one day, Danny and Tycho ran around saying "drang" to Mom and Dad and Grandma. They taught it to their friends, who repeated it to their parents. It was sweet to see our two little brothers getting along so well.

But saying "drang" produced no satisfying response; nobody was shocked and horrified. Soon they knew we had tricked them. It was their first scientific experiment. Our credibility was destroyed.

Danny and Tycho were very clever. They went right back to saying all the other words, and there was nothing we could do about it.

Frank's Mother

When I was in sixth grade, my best friend was a kid named Frank. We hung out at my house a lot more than his. One reason for this was that both my parents worked—Mom was a pediatrician and Dad was a physiology professor at the university—and after school there would always be several hours at my house when no adults would be around. Frank, knowing his mother was watching the clock for his return, would dutifully call her as soon as we got to my place and tell her where he was (without, of course, mentioning that my mother wasn't there). Then we could do what we wanted.

We stood on the back porch railing and peed out into the yard. We studied the color photographs in my mother's medical books. Some of the pictures, of hideous skin diseases, for instance, were thrillingly gross, giving us weird pangs in our stomachs. Other pictures were fascinating for different reasons.

We played catch with eggs. There was a lot of tension to this game because we were both lousy athletes, and we knew that it would not be long before an egg would smash on the floor or on the kitchen counter. Then we would scrape the egg into a big bowl and make fake vomit. We'd dump in oatmeal, brown sugar, vinegar, syrup, raspberry jam (for bloodiness), and whatever else seemed disgustingly realistic. When we were satisfied with our artistry, we would splash the mixture onto the sidewalk in front of the house. Then, hiding on the front porch, we'd watch the reactions of passersby, praying that someone would step in it.

Even when Mom did come home, it was still fun at my house because she was very relaxed and did not fuss over her kids. She had her own things to do and would leave us alone. Frank and I would go up to my room, which was a refinished attic—we lived in a big old house, and I had the whole top floor to myself—where we could read comics and use bad language and have private conversations about anything we wanted.

Mom was unconventional in many ways. She let my sister and brothers and me read anything we wanted and never objected to any of our friends or quizzed us about where we were when we weren't at home. She thought it was great that I loved puppets and loathed baseball. She never tried to make us finish our food at meals, which was probably why none of us ever had any eating problems. Though Mom was proud of her Jewish heritage—her mother and father were poor immigrants from the Warsaw ghetto—neither of our parents was religious. Many kids we knew went to synagogue or Sunday school; we never attended any religious services. On Sunday mornings (Dad worked on Saturdays), the whole family had a large, leisurely breakfast together, while Dad played chamber music on the phonograph.

Since Mom was a pediatrician, I never entered a doctor's office until I went away to college. Mom gave us all our shots, and none of us was the least bit afraid of the needle. In fact, a couple of times Mom took Vicky to her clinic. She gathered the kids around and gave Vicky a shot of some innocuous substance while Vicky stood there beaming, to try to prove to the other kids that it didn't hurt.

Mom did not wear high heels or makeup, which was very unusual in those days. "Why should you worry about what some stranger thinks about you?" she would ask us. But she wasn't obnoxiously rigid about this. When Vicky was a little girl, she would beg Mom to *please* wear lipstick whenever she came to school, and Mom would oblige, not wanting to embarrass her.

Sometimes Frank and I did have to go over to his house because his mother had this idea that it somehow wasn't fair for us to spend all our time at my house. We also didn't want her to get suspicious and start wondering exactly *why* we so preferred my house to his. His mother would be waiting for us at the door of their ranch house—in a dress and stockings and high heels, her hair in a permanent, her face perfectly made up—and she would always be holding a tray of donuts or jelly rolls or cookies. We would have to sit with her at the kitchen table and force down the sugary pastries and drink glass after glass of milk, while she questioned us in her ladylike way about what had happened at school.

She would also ask politely about my family—how my sister was doing, and my two little brothers. Frank was an only child, which might have accounted for his mother's relentless hovering. I suppose she was impressed that my father was a scientist at the university, but though she refrained from comment about my mother's profession, it was clear that she did not approve of a mother who worked. I did manage to imply, however, that Mom only worked part-time and of course was *always* there when I came home from school.

When the snack ordeal was over, we could not escape up to Frank's room—that was out of bounds because his mother couldn't keep an eye on us there. We would have to sit, squirming with boredom, in the formal, spotlessly clean living room. All the furniture was covered in transparent plastic, which was either slippery or sticky, depending on the weather, and always uncomfortable. Frank's mother bustled around, vacuuming, polishing, dusting the plastic flowers, frequently peeking in to see what we were doing. Not that there was anything interesting we *could* do. I would never stay very long. My visits there were the price we had to pay for the freedom we enjoyed at my house.

Things continued in this way without mishap for most of sixth grade. Then, toward the end of the school year, I made a fatal blunder: I invited Frank to sleep over.

It was going to be a great night, a Saturday. Two of our other friends were coming; there was plenty of space in my large attic room for sleeping bags. Vicky would be sleeping at someone else's house, so she wouldn't be in our hair. I knew my parents would leave us alone—and they had said I could bring the TV up to the top floor; we could watch the kind of late movies they showed when kids were usually asleep. I had also just discovered two very lavishly illustrated new books in Mom's medical library, which I knew everyone would find deeply fascinating. And since the attic was pretty well soundproofed, we'd be able to stay up all night if we wanted.

Frank was torn. He desperately wanted to come. But it was a certainty that his mother would not allow him to spend the night without first checking all the details with my mother. So far, our mothers had never met or even spoken on the phone, and we wanted to keep it that way.

"If I ask her, she'll call your mother up," Frank told me miserably after school on Friday. "She'll ask her all sorts of questions, like if they're going to keep an eye on us and make us go to bed early and stuff like that. And what if she finds out your mother isn't there after school? I'll never be able to come over again."

"Maybe I can get my mother to say they'll make us go to bed early. And maybe she just won't tell her how late she works," I said, not too sure about this. But it was worth a try. The party wouldn't be the same without Frank and his crazy sense of humor. And he was my best friend. "She wouldn't be lying, exactly. I'll ask her first, then call you."

But as loose as Mom was, she had her limits. "Poor Frank," she said. "His mother sounds like a pill. I guess I can *imply* that you'll be supervised. But I can't lie to her about how late I work. She's his mother; she has a right to know the situation. Anyway, what would someone like that do if she found *out* I lied to her? I dread to think."

"I'm not asking you to lie. Just don't tell her. And if she asks, be vague."

I called Frank, and then we put our mothers on the phone. I listened nervously to our end of the conversation. "I can assure you, the boys won't get into any mischief," Mom said in her most businesslike voice. "Billy's had friends over before; it's always been fine. And we'll certainly see to it that they don't stay up late—we'll want our sleep, too." There was a pause. I held my breath, wondering what Frank's mother was asking now. "Yes, there'll be plenty of healthy food for them to eat; I know what growing boys are like." Another pause. Mom rolled her eyes at me. "I *did* study nutrition in medical school," she said, a slight edge to her voice. "You know Billy's not underfed. And he hasn't missed a day of school all year."

She hung up with an expression of disgust. "That poor kid," she said again. "But I think I convinced her. She's dropping him off at five-thirty. A little early, but that's okay."

I was excited and happy all day on Saturday, setting up my room, eager for the time to pass quickly. At four-thirty the doorbell rang, I pulled open the front door—and my heart sank. Frank's mother had *not* just dropped him off. She was standing there beside him, dressed as though she were going to tea with the queen, obviously expecting to be invited in. Frank did not look very happy.

"Hello, Billy," his mother said, with her tight, artificial smile—I wondered how she could smile even *that* much, with all the makeup she had on. "I just wanted to come in for a minute and have a little chat with your mom."

"Uh, sure, come in," I said, wishing I had been warned about this, thinking fast, trying to avert disaster.

His mother's high heels clicked across the wooden floors—her house, of course, had wall-to-wall carpeting. I walked ahead of her; Frank trailed behind. I stopped in the living room and turned back. Frank's mother was looking around at the forest of houseplants, the old Oriental rugs, the dragon-legged library table piled with magazines. "Listen, why don't you just sit down in here," I said. "And I'll go get my mother. She's, uh, busy in the kitchen."

"Oh, let's not be formal about this," Frank's mother said, though she was the one who was all dressed up. "And I don't want to interrupt her cooking. I'll just pop in and say hi."

"But . . ." I tried to protest.

"The kitchen must be this way," Frank's mother said, heading right for it. There was nothing I could do.

Mom was sitting at the kitchen table feeding the baby, who was two months old. She wore an ancient, faded housedress and was barefoot, her legs unshaven.

"Mom, this is Frank's mother," I mumbled.

"Very nice to meet you," Frank's mother said, her eyes moving between the dirty dishes in the sink and the piles of soil on the kitchen table from the plants Mom had been repotting. Mom was a good housekeeper, and we also had a cleaning woman during the week. But on Saturdays Mom relaxed.

"Oh, hello," Mom said, a little surprised, glancing at me, then at Frank's mother. "Pull up a chair for her, Billy."

Frank's mother sat down gingerly on the edge of the chair, as though protecting her dress from its surface. "Hello there, honey," she said to the baby in an artificial voice. "And what's *your* name?"

Mom gazed fondly at the baby. "He doesn't have a name. I suppose we'll have to come up with one eventually."

Frank's mother looked blank, as though the concept of a baby without a name was beyond her comprehension. She glanced around uncomfortably. "What a big old house you have. It must be very time-consuming, keeping it . . ." Then she stopped, not wanting to say the wrong thing.

"It works for us," Mom said, not too warmly, since she had caught the implication that her house wasn't clean.

Frank's mother tried again. "I hear your husband is a scientist."

"A physiologist. He does experiments on live human heart muscle," Mom told her.

"*Live* human heart muscle?" Frank's mother said. "But where does he get live—"

Vicky and her friend Avis dashed into the kitchen, giggling. They had dyed their hair purple with grape juice; their teeth were colored red, white, and blue with lipstick and eye makeup; and their clothes were smeared with various unidentifiable substances. "Are there any cookies left, Mom?" Vicky demanded.

"No. Anyway, it's too close to supper to eat stuff like that. Have an apple if you're hungry."

Finally, Mom was saying something vaguely normal. But when Vicky took the apple from the bowl on the counter, it slipped out of her hand and rolled across the floor—which, due to potting soil, was not what anyone would call clean. Vicky picked the apple up from the floor and immediately bit into it, and she and Avis raced out of the room.

"But she didn't *wash* it!" Frank's mother could not keep herself from expostulating.

Mom shrugged. She was not pleased by Frank's mother's remark. "It's good for them to eat food off the floor. Dirt builds up immunities. I never wash food, never sterilized a bottle in my life. And my kids are never sick."

I couldn't really blame Mom. If she'd known Frank's mother was actually coming inside, she would have kept her out of the messy kitchen; she might have made an effort to fix up her appearance a little. But this woman had arrived early, invaded her house without warning, and pushed her way into the kitchen. It was too late now for Mom to put on a false front.

I already knew there was no hope of Frank spending the night or even eating over here again. His mother would certainly not want him to be exposed to any food that was not sterile. And it was clear that Mom was not paying any attention to what Vicky and Avis were doing, which meant she would also not be supervising us tonight. It was only a matter of time until Frank's mother dragged him home—and I was hoping it would be soon, before anything else happened.

A vain hope. Danny, who was almost two and a half, tottered into the kitchen, sucking his thumb.

Frank's mother was still trying to maintain a pleasant facade. She smiled at Danny. "Aren't you adorable," she said, in the same artificial voice she had used with the baby. "But you know, it's not good to suck your thumb, dear."

Danny looked puzzled and slowly took his thumb out of his mouth.

Mom was really fed up. "Danny," she said, "put your thumb *back* in your mouth."

Danny comfortably obeyed.

At last Frank's mother had had enough. She stood up. "Well, thank you for inviting us in," she said. "Now it's time for us to go. It's been a very, uh, *interesting* visit."

"Isn't Frank spending the night?" Mom asked her, as though she didn't already know the answer. "Oops," she casually added, as a fountain of baby vomit splashed onto the table.

"Not, uh, this time, I'm afraid," Frank's mother said. I could see the struggle she was having not to rush from the room. "Good afternoon."

I followed them to the door. "Bye, Frank," I said sadly.

He just looked at me. I didn't envy him. He was going to have a lot of questions to answer now.

The next year, Frank was sent to a fancy private school, and I attended public junior high. It was only natural that we soon stopped seeing each other. It turned out, years later, that we both went to Harvard. But we did not renew our friendship. By then, Frank had become a preppie and was part of a super-conformist clique—the kind of people I would have nothing to do with and who, of course, wouldn't be seen dead with someone like me.

But I sometimes wondered: Would he have turned out differently if his mother had *not* come into the house that afternoon?

The Freedom Fighters of Parkview

The Greenbergs often came to our house for Thanksgiving dinner and other holidays. The parents were both highly respected literary scholars. They were also urbane and bawdy and were the only other parents we knew who seemed just as easygoing and relaxed with their kids as our parents were.

Vicky and I always loved it when the Greenbergs came over because we had so much fun with their kids. Vera was three years older than me, Nick a year younger than Vera; both were brainy and good-looking. They were popular at school, though not the least bit pituh.

Pituh was a term that Vicky and her friends Avis and Eleanor had coined to describe the members of the pop-

ular cliques at junior high and high school. That Vera
and Nick were popular *without* being pituh was a unique
combination of attributes, and Vicky and I both looked
up to them. It would have been natural for us to resent
them, since Mom was always telling us what brilliant
students they were, so athletic, attractive, articulate, and
so on. But we couldn't help liking them anyway (though
Vicky would often scream at Mom to shut up about
them). Vera and Nick also clearly enjoyed spending time
with us on these family occasions, though we couldn't
really be friends with them at school, since they were
older and hung out with a different crowd.

It was the Greenberg kids who taught us to play the
card game I Doubt It. The basic object of the game was
to cheat. We loved it. There were many moments during
I Doubt It when you'd try to scream furiously at somebody but couldn't manage it because you were laughing
too hard.

On Thanksgiving, when I was in seventh grade, we
couldn't play I Doubt It because many of the cards had
disappeared. Danny, who was four, denied any knowl-
edge of them. We discovered what remained of the missing cards when Mom made Vicky change Tycho.
Confronted with this palpable evidence, Danny admitted
that he had fed them to him. Both sets of parents thought
this was very funny.

But Vicky and I felt it was unfair that Danny had not even been chastised for ruining our game. The Greenberg kids were disappointed, too. And so, instead of playing I Doubt It, we sat around in my third-floor room, complaining about adults in general and our parents in particular. It was our first conversation of this kind with the Greenberg kids.

Of course, both sets of parents, merely by existing, had certain defects in common. All parents, by definition, were arbitrary, unfair, demanding, and constitutionally incapable of understanding their children or of seeing any point of view but their own. This was nothing new. But kids from each family were fascinated to discover how many previously unimagined tortures the *other* set of parents routinely inflicted on their children. Vicky and I were particularly surprised and gratified to find out that the Greenberg parents did not think their kids were as perfect as our mother did—far from it.

"Your parents really force you to *eat*?" I gasped in wonder.

"You mean yours *don't*?" Nick replied.

Vicky and I shook our heads.

Vera nodded grimly. "We don't leave the table until we finish as much as they decide to dish out. And if they catch us with anything like chocolate, then it's pimple-inspection time." She rolled her eyes.

Vicky and I were shocked. "But you guys don't have pimples," I said. "Our mother goes on and on about what flawless complexions you have."

"She does?"

"She's always talking about how wonderful and perfect you are, how much better than us," Vicky said. "Not that we hold it against you or anything," she added quickly. "She does it with other people's kids, too. Her favorite topic is how much worse we are than all her friends' kids."

Vera and Nick clucked sympathetically. "Well, at least she doesn't do it in public," Vera said consolingly. "Our mother's always telling people the most personal, embarrassing things about us while we're sitting right there. It makes me want to sink through the floor."

Now Vicky and I made sympathetic noises. Vera, who was efficient and well organized, began to make a list of our parents' various sins against us. She was the oldest and the most practiced at taking notes in school—no one else could have written fast enough to get it all down legibly.

Mom found the list of parental outrages the next day when she went up to my room to make my bed. She was not in the best mood, since she and Vicky had just had a screaming fight, and Vicky was sulking in her room. Mom caught sight of Vera's notes on my bedside table, two wailing toddlers pulling and clawing relentlessly at her as she struggled to plump my pillows and straighten my sheets.

I was lying on the couch downstairs, reading a wonderful book of horror stories Mom had recently given me, enjoying the rich aroma of the turkey soup, which had already been simmering on the stove when I got up that morning. I was so engrossed in Lovecraft's "The Dunwich Horror" that I didn't even notice Mom's approach, despite the pervasive stench of Tycho's loaded diaper, which inevitably accompanied her. Only when Mom said, "Is this Vera's handwriting?" did I look up.

She was standing above me, holding Tycho against her hip with one arm and Vera's notes in her other hand. My first response, when I realized an already irate Mom had read the list, was chillier than anything evoked by the Lovecraft story.

"Vera's handwriting?" I said stupidly. "Oh, um . . . I guess . . . I mean . . ."

But Mom chuckled. "This has got to be one of the funniest things I've ever seen in my life. Listen to this." And she read, " 'In the privacy of their home, the parents drop their fake public behavior and reveal their true natures: disgusting slobs who laze around the house, reprimanding their kids the instant they are not industrious, engaged in constructive behavior, or impeccably groomed.' "

"Nick said that, not me or Vicky," I quickly pointed out.

"Of course *you* dumbbells didn't," Mom said. "The Greenberg kids are clever enough to come up with something that has a real comic punch to it."

I had finally realized she wasn't angry; now *I* was insulted. "But we *were* the ones who said parents are always telling their own kids how inferior they are to other people's children."

"I know you have a talent for inventing things, Billy. But that remark just isn't as witty as Nick's. Sorry."

I didn't know what to say.

"Take Tycho and clean him up," she told me. "I want to look this over again."

"You've already read the whole thing?"

"Uh-huh." She thrust Tycho at me. He started screaming the instant I lifted him, very carefully, from Mom's hip. She sank down on the couch with Vera's notes as I bore him away.

I didn't really worry that the Greenberg kids might get in trouble as a result of Mom's finding the list. Mom was not the kind of unscrupulous person who would cause problems by reporting anything from the notes directly to the Greenberg parents. Her discovery of the list had quite different repercussions.

I don't remember whose idea it was to turn the notes into a play about the horrors inflicted by adults—especially parents—onto children. What I do know is that Mom was the driving force behind the entire production. She worked harder on it than anybody else, even though she had a full-time job and Danny and Tycho to deal with.

The first meeting took place the Saturday after Thanksgiving. The industrious, well-groomed, and witty Greenberg kids were there, of course. We also invited Albert, who was Vera's age, and Vicky's friends Avis and Eleanor, and my friends Nicole and Bart and Matilda.

The initial brainstorming session did not begin well. Some of the kids were understandably constrained by Mom's presence—she *was* a member of the enemy camp, after all—and did not dare to express themselves freely. Mom attacked this problem by reading the list aloud herself, praising much of it, and contributing her own creative and constructive suggestions for improvement. It became apparent to everyone that Mom was being completely objective and not taking any of the material personally.

It *was* a little disconcerting that Mom had to stop reading at frequent intervals because she was laughing so hard. Unlike the rest of us, she seemed to consider our list a source of hilarity, rather than a cause for righteous indignation. "*This* line will have them rolling in the aisles," she said, more than once.

Mom also made it clear that she would not say a word

about the play to any of the other parents. Her statement had credibility because everyone knew she had not mentioned the list to the adult Greenbergs, as any other parent would have done. Anyway, it was obvious that Mom did not take the list very seriously. She seemed to think it was mostly invention or exaggeration—even the parts about her, oddly enough, things that Vicky and I knew she had done. But because of her relaxed attitude, all the kids soon began loosening up. It helped that our house was a popular hangout, a familiar place where kids were already comfortable, mainly because Mom was so easygoing and unconcerned about things like hygiene, foul language, and personal appearance—matters other parents were so unreasonably fussy about.

Again, Vera took notes. Before the session was over, we had so much great material that we knew already we had a show. We decided on a date for the performance, a Saturday in January, at this first meeting.

We met once a week. A series of scenes began to develop. We didn't write out the dialogue word for word; we would set up a situation and then let the actors improvise within it. Vera and Albert, being the oldest and most mature in appearance, took on with relish the villainous roles of the parents. The others, except for me, mostly played the heroic children. I was the pianist—this was turning out to be a musical production—and I represented the Spirit of Childhood. I was something akin to a Greek chorus, reflecting in my music and demeanor the emotional states of the protagonists. I was also the stagehand, turning the lights on and off to indicate scene changes.

By now, all the kids knew that Mom had kept her promise—if she'd said one thing about the contents of the play to their parents, they would have heard about it. It seemed quite natural that Mom became the director; everyone had to admit that she was essential to the production. She participated with such vitality and spirit, stimulating enthusiasm in the cast, and her lyrics were so inventive and trenchant.

It was Mom who came up with the name of our theatrical group, The Parkview Traumatic Club—Parkview was the name of our suburb—and also the title for the production itself. The courageous and ultimately doomed Hungarian Freedom Fighters were big news at the time, and so calling our show *The Freedom Fighters of Parkview* gave it significance.

The stage was the front hall of our house. The piano was there, and the front hall had direct access to the kitchen, which functioned as the dressing room. The hall was also the only room in the house that had an overhead light fixture and could be darkened or illuminated by the flick of a single switch. The audience—teenage friends of the actors, parents of the cast, and other adults whose children were not in the show—sat on rows of chairs in the living room.

My role gave me more opportunity than the others to observe the reactions of the audience.

The play began with Vicky seated at the breakfast table, neatly dressed in a skirt and blouse, her hair impeccably groomed (for the first and last time in years). A huge stack of barely thawed pancakes towered on a plate in front of her, and next to it sat a gallon container of milk with a straw protruding from the top. She was trying to eat her way through this gargantuan meal.

Vera, as her mother, lounged at the table in curlers and a dirty bathrobe, smoking and nibbling candy. "Another slow day, I see," she said, looking at the height of the pancake pile. "Marylou Pinsky always cleans her plate right away. But *you* force me to sit here and remind you that you're not getting up from this table until you finish your breakfast down to the last drop and crumb."

"Mother, I can see the school bus coming," the daughter nervously whispered—she had choked down only half the pancakes. "If I miss it, I'll get in trouble at school for being late again."

"Excuses, excuses." The mother studied a piece of candy for awhile. "And don't bother asking *me* to write you a note for being late. You have to learn to take responsibility for your actions."

At the end of the scene, the daughter waddled from the table, her stomach grotesquely distended. (The pillow stuffed into her blouse had been invisible to the audience while she was seated.) I switched off the ceiling light with a mournful expression. There was a lot of applause. The set change took several minutes, but the audience was still laughing when we had finished. I glanced curiously at the Greenberg parents. Mrs. Greenberg seemed a little self-conscious.

In every scene, the children were angelic, the adults inhumanly cruel. As Mom had predicted, the audience loved it. But despite the continued enthusiastic applause after each episode, I was a little nervous about the next-to-last scene, an evening at home. This scene was almost entirely based on material from the Greenberg kids—material that Mom assumed was grossly exaggerated, if not imaginary.

The two children, Nick and Vicky, sat at the table doing their homework. They were neatly dressed and perfectly groomed.

The mother, still in curlers and bathrobe, sprawled on the couch, watching TV and chain-smoking, picking sullenly at candy between cigarettes. The father, in a dirty undershirt, sat at the other end of the couch, swilling down beer. The parents had a bitter conversation about how inferior their children were to the brilliant, good-looking, and well-behaved children of their friends. The mother got on the phone and complained about her children to several of her friends, while the father read a cheap paperback novel with a lurid cover.

Suddenly the father exploded—he had noticed his daughter was reading a book of poems by Edna St. Vincent Millay. "Filthy trash!" he shouted, as he tore the book in half and threw it to the floor.

And then he peered more closely at the daughter for a long, tense moment. "Oh, my God," he said in a choked voice. "Is it possible? And yet . . . I see it."

"See what, Father?" the daughter said, obviously afraid of what was coming next.

He closed his eyes and swallowed deeply, as though speech were almost beyond him. "A *pimple!*" he breathed.

Mrs. Greenberg laughed so loudly and so long at this point that the action had to be delayed. This time, I noticed, it was Mr. Greenberg who seemed a little embarrassed.

"No, Father, please. You must be mistaken," the daughter protested, turning her head away from him in an automatic response of self-protection. "I checked my face really carefully, right after I washed the dishes and mopped the floor. There was nothing, I promise."

"You expect me to ignore the evidence of my own eyes?" cried the father, whipping a magnifying glass from his pocket. "And don't cringe!" he ordered her. He lifted her head roughly by the chin, bent over, and scrutinized her face through the powerful magnifying lens as she tried not to squirm. "There it is, just as I thought." He jabbed her cheek with one finger. "Right there, in the upper left quadrant. What have I told you about proper hygiene? Upstairs, to the bathroom," he pronounced in righteous tones. "Do not come out until you've spent the next hour with your pimple soap and pimple pads and pimple creams and pimple powder—and all your other pimple crap!"

The daughter hid her head in her hands and ran from the room.

I staggered over to turn off the light, my face a mask of pain. This time the laughter went on for so long that I had to stand there, waiting for it to die away, before I could switch on the light. But when I did, I stood up straight again, radiating health, smiling benignly. Things had begun to change.

It was a revolutionary cell, where the children were hard at work cleaning and loading guns, moving sandbags (represented by bed pillows), and checking and rechecking lists. Devoted comrades, they shared equally in the work, hurrying to help one another whenever it was necessary.

Vicky was the revolutionary leader, in a quasi-military beret and oversized boots. Though her character had suffered more at the hands of parents than any of the others, she was also the most temperate, cautioning her comrades to base their cause on empathy and reason rather than crude emotion. "We can't allow ourselves to sink to their level," she urged the other freedom fighters. "Remember to shoot into the air. Our object is not to kill or maim, but to achieve our rightful independence. The weapons are just a means of gaining control. Only through nonviolence can true justice prevail."

"Even though they have perpetrated such gross abuses of human rights?" someone objected.

"Remember, they too must once have been human beings like ourselves, hard as it is to believe," Vicky said gently. "Our goal is not to repeat their mistakes, but to guide them by our own example. Only through education will they learn the error of their ways."

"But exactly what will we do with them once we *are* in power?" the others wanted to know.

"Nursing homes, of course," Vicky said.

Again, Vicky had to wait for the audience to stop laughing. Finally she had to shout to be heard. "The time is at hand!" she announced. "To your battle stations. Soon victory will be ours! Remember, we have nothing to lose but our chains."

The freedom fighters briefly clasped hands. Then they separated and moved to crouch in various positions about the stage. They waited, their eyes all on Vicky. She checked and rechecked her watch.

At last she lifted her arm in preparation to give the signal to begin their heroic struggle for liberation.

At that moment, the mother rushed on. "So there you are!" she cried shrilly. "You're late for supper again! You'll pay for this. And don't snivel!" She grabbed Vicky by the ear and pulled her off the stage, toppling the revolution before it had even begun.

I barely managed to crawl from the piano to turn off the light, ending the show.

While we were taking our bows, Nick darted unexpectedly into the kitchen and pulled a protesting Mom, who had helped with the costume changes during the show, onto the stage. Vera produced a large bouquet of roses.

"We would all like to express our heartfelt thanks to Dr. Esther Kaplan Sleator," Vera said, smiling warmly at Mom as she presented her with the flowers. "Without her inspiration and tireless effort, none of this would have been possible." (It was, Mom told us later, exactly the kind of thoughtful gesture she would expect the Greenberg kids to come up with.)

The audience applauded appreciatively after Vera's little speech. The Greenberg parents clapped just as much as the others—though I also noticed that they were whispering together, their eyes on Mom.

We had dinner at the Greenbergs' house a few weeks

later. Mrs. Greenberg smoked and described how Vera's devoted boyfriend picked her up every morning in a huge Cadillac that was a particularly hideous shade of pink. "The color makes you want to vomit!" exclaimed Vera's mother, the famous scholar, laughing as she put out her cigarette in a full ashtray.

She also talked about how Nick, who was on the swim team, always made sure to do his body-building exercises immediately before appearing in public in his swimsuit. Nick quickly left the room, ostensibly to get his father another beer. He had a very noticeable patch of some kind of cream on his forehead, and his skin looked a bit raw.

Mom was unusually quiet at the Greenbergs' that night, as though puzzled about something. She was, I seem to remember, almost silent as we drove home. For the first time in my memory, she did not go on and on about how great the Greenberg kids were.

But it only lasted that night. The next day she was back to normal again.

The Hypnotist

When Danny was in grade school, his best friend was a boy named Jack. They seemed to be total opposites.

Danny was a rapid-fire talker, full of nervous energy, always doing something with his hands. Jack was dreamy and vague. Whenever Mom picked him up at his house, she always had to wait interminably for him to make his way down the front walk to the car. "Good old Jack, slower than molasses in January," Mom would say, resignedly turning off the ignition.

It took Jack so long to answer a question that you wondered if he'd even heard it. And when he finally did respond in his flat, toneless voice, there were such

prolonged gaps between words, even between syllables, that he might have been speaking in a foreign
language. He spent a lot of time staring vacantly into
space.

But he wasn't stupid. It was Jack who noticed the
advertisement in the back pages of a comic book: *Teach
yourself hypnosis. Complete course in one simple, easy-
to-read pamphlet. Only twenty-five cents. Money-back
guarantee. Enclose self-addressed stamped envelope with
each order.* It was Jack who addressed and mailed the
envelope. It was Jack who read the pamphlet from cover
to cover, learning the instructions.

And it was Jack who tested it out—on Tycho.

Geneva, the cleaning woman, was busy downstairs.
Mom and Dad were at work, I was at my summer job,
and Vicky was somewhere with friends. Jack's mother
had dropped him off at our house after lunch; Mom would
take him home when she got back from work.

Tycho was eight, two years younger than Danny and
Jack, and he felt honored to be included by the older
boys in one of their activities. More important, he knew
that Danny would not leave him alone until he agreed
to whatever Danny wanted. And Danny, of course, rel-
ished the idea of Tycho being the guinea pig.

Jack gently ushered Tycho into Danny's room. It was
a rare privilege for Tycho to be allowed into this room at

all. Danny usually kept him out, for fear that he might accidentally damage one of Danny's projects, such as the delicate and complicated model airplane Danny had been working on for weeks and had just completed that morning.

Jack had threaded a piece of string through a foil-wrapped chocolate coin. He sat Tycho comfortably down on a chair, meticulously pulled the window shades down, one by one, turned off the light, and told Danny to focus a flashlight beam on the coin.

"Keep your eyes on the coin," Jack instructed Tycho in his level, emotionless voice, swinging the coin slowly back and forth. "Focus all your attention on the coin. . . . There is nothing else . . . nothing but the coin. . . . You are so comfortable, so relaxed, so sleepy. . . . Your eyelids are growing heavy. . . . You can't keep them open now. . . . All you want is sleep . . . deep and restful sleep . . ."

There was enough light for Danny and Jack to see Tycho's eyelids flutter and then slowly close. "You are deeply asleep now . . . but you can still hear my voice," Jack said. "Are you asleep now?"

"Yes," Tycho uttered, in a voice nearly as flat and expressionless as Jack's.

"Okay. Turn on the light, Danny," Jack said, so cool and matter-of-fact that he might have successfully achieved this scientific result dozens of times before.

Danny flipped on the light and then hurried over to Tycho, eagerly bending down to study his face. Tycho's eyes remained closed, his arms hanging at his sides in the straight-backed chair. Danny turned quickly back to Jack. "You think he's really hypnotized?" he asked him in an excited whisper, rubbing his hands together. "He's not faking it or anything?"

"We'll find out," Jack said blandly. He took one careful, measured step toward Tycho and stood staring down at him for a long moment, thinking.

"Well? Is he?" Danny said, hopping with impatience.

Jack ignored him, watching Tycho. Finally he said, "Tycho, your arms are tied to your sides by a very strong rope. The rope is very tight, wrapped around you many times, and you can't reach back to untie it. Can you feel the rope?"

"Uh-huh," Tycho said, nodding slightly, pressing his arms against his body.

"You can't move your arms, no matter how hard you try. Can you move your arms?"

Tycho's arms quivered. His body tensed. "No, I . . . I can't," he replied, with a slight frown.

"But . . . your nose itches. It itches something terrible. You can't stand it for another second," Jack mildly informed him.

Tycho's nose twitched. His hands clenched; his shoulders tightened. Gradually, veins stood out on his arms as he strained, trembling, to move them. They wouldn't move. His forehead creased; his cheeks flushed with effort. He grunted.

Danny's eyes lit up. He looked at Jack, then Tycho, then at Jack again—who was watching Tycho dispassionately.

Suddenly Danny's face fell. "He's faking it; he's *got* to be!" he exclaimed. "You're faking it, Tycho, you jerk!" he accused him, lifting his fist threateningly.

Tycho didn't notice. He went on struggling miserably to move his arms, sweat breaking out on his forehead.

"Tycho, the rope is gone," Jack said quietly.

Tycho's hands shot to his nose, furiously scratching. His shoulders sagged in relief.

"He's faking it," Danny said. "I know what he's like. This is boring." He sighed and scowled at Tycho.

Tycho continued scratching ferociously. Jack wandered over to Danny's desk, picked up the hypnotism pamphlet, and paged through it in a leisurely manner.

Tycho's fingernails tore more wildly at the skin of his nose.

"Hey, I think his nose is starting to bleed," Danny said, no longer so skeptical.

"Umm," Jack murmured, slowly turning a page. "Oh,

yeah . . . that one." He studied the pamphlet a moment longer, then finally closed it and carefully positioned it on the desk beside Danny's beloved plane, staring thoughtfully down at the booklet for a while.

"His nose *is* bleeding," Danny said, sounding worried. "Maybe you better do something before he hurts himself."

Jack turned vaguely toward Tycho. "Huh? Oh. Okay, the itch is gone, Tycho."

Tycho let his hands fall limply to his sides, seemingly unaware of the drop of blood that dangled from the tip of his inflamed nose and then dropped down onto his chin.

"But now . . . you are thirsty." Jack plodded back toward Tycho. "You haven't had any water in days . . . days and days. You've never been so thirsty in your life. Your mouth feels like it's stuffed with cotton. Oh, yeah . . . Your arms are tied to your sides again. And you can open your eyes now."

Tycho's arms stiffened. His eyelids lifted; he stared blankly at nothing. His lips parted slightly, bits of them sticking together. The tip of his tongue emerged, moving slowly back and forth.

"You are dying for a drink of water; the thirst is killing you," Jack recited in a monotone, as though reading from a book.

48

Tycho's throat contracted with a sick, rasping choke.

"You will do anything for a drink. But," Jack mentioned, "your hands are still tied. You can't turn on a faucet or pick up a glass. And you are dying of thirst. You are so thirsty that—"

Even Jack was startled when Tycho bounded from the chair and dashed out of the room. Danny raced after him, and Jack actually managed to sort of lope along behind.

They found Tycho in the bathroom, kneeling beside the toilet, his head thrust deep into the bowl, his arms at his sides. His mouth was immersed in the water, making gurgling and splashing sounds as he desperately lapped and gulped it down. He kept it up until Jack granted Tycho the information that his thirst was quenched. Tycho immediately pulled his head out of the toilet bowl.

"I guess he's not faking it," Danny had to admit when they were all back in his room, Tycho docilely seated in the chair again.

"There's a final proof," Jack said, after taking his time to consult the pamphlet once more. "Okay, Tycho, listen carefully," he instructed him. "After I wake you up, you will forget everything that happened while you were asleep—except one thing. Whenever anybody says the word *window*, you will pick up the nearest object you can find and throw it to the floor. Do you understand?"

Tycho nodded.

"You will forget everything that happened except for that one instruction. Okay?"

"Okay," Tycho repeated.

"Now I'm going to count to three," Jack said. "And when I say 'three,' you will be fully awake. Here we go. One . . . two . . . three."

Tycho blinked. His eyes focused on Jack, then on Danny. "Why did you turn the light back on?" he asked. "Aren't you going to hypnotize me?"

Tycho was confused when Danny burst into laughter. "What's so funny?" he wanted to know. "I don't get it. Why didn't you hypnotize me?"

"We just decided not to," Danny said. "Jack, I think you should open the *window* shades."

Tycho stood up, walked over to Danny's desk, picked up the beautiful model plane, and hurled it to the floor, smashing it to pieces.

Danny did not share Jack's mild amusement. "Tycho!" he howled. "How could . . . Why did . . ." He smacked Tycho hard across the face, then sank mournfully to the floor, gathering up the ruined plane.

Tycho put his hand to his cheek. But he seemed more upset about the plane than the slap. "I'm sorry, Danny," he cried, on the verge of tears because of the terrible thing he had done. "I don't know what happened! *Really*. All of a sudden I just *had* to do it."

"You're faking it!" Danny screamed at him. "You're just pretending it was because . . ." He bit his lip, looking down at the plane again, wondering.

"Danny, something *made* me do it," Tycho piteously and hopelessly persisted. "I don't understand it. I'm so sorry. Please believe me. I know it sounds crazy. But . . . but . . ."

"Forget it, Tycho," Danny snarled at him in frustration. He glared up at Jack. "If he's *not* faking it, then it's your fault," he said. "Maybe you better—"

"Come on now, kids! Time for Jack to go home," Mom called from downstairs. She had just come back from a long, hot day at work, and her tone of voice indicated that she was not to be argued with. "And would you try to hurry, for a change? I've got a lot of things to do."

Danny and Tycho went along for the ride, Tycho in the front seat. Danny fuming and Jack smiling remotely to himself in the back. As Mom irritably waited while Jack made his way up the front walk, she said, "It's hot, Tycho; roll down the window."

Tycho grabbed Mom's handbag, sitting open beside her on the seat, and threw it to the floor of the car, scattering most of its contents.

"Tycho, you monster!" Mom screamed. "Are you *nuts*? Pick it all up this instant!"

Tycho obeyed immediately, not holding back his tears now. Danny wasn't amused this time either.

They were both abnormally quiet during supper. The rest of the family chatted away as usual.

Mom talked about her job. She was a pediatrician for the public health department, working in free clinics for poor people in the inner city. "A woman came in today who lives in that terrible Pruitt–Igo project," she was saying. "She has five kids and lives in a two-room apartment on the eleventh floor. She has to keep her kids inside all day long because of the toughs in the playground. Even if she could watch them from the window, she wouldn't be able to—"

Tycho picked up his plate of spaghetti with meat sauce and smashed it on the floor. Mom shrieked; Tycho wailed in apparent bewilderment.

It was Dad, who could usually be counted on to remain calm in moments of stress, who noticed how uncomfortably Danny was cringing in his chair. It was Dad who patiently got the whole story out of Danny. Mom had wiped the spaghetti sauce off the floor and served dessert by the time Danny finished.

"Well, can't we just hypnotize him again and tell him not to do it anymore?" Dad asked him.

"I think it will only work if Jack does it," Danny said. "He's the one who hypnotized him and gave him the suggestion. And . . . he didn't say anything about how to make Tycho stop doing it. Maybe . . . he *can't* stop," Danny added in a hushed voice.

"But Jack *didn't* hypnotize me," Tycho insisted. "Nothing happened. I didn't drink water out of the toilet. I'd never do *that!*"

"If that's the case, then you must be making these messes on purpose," Mom accused him.

"But why would I get in trouble on purpose?" Tycho asked her, sounding completely innocent.

"Tycho just doesn't remember being hypnotized because Jack told him not to," Danny explained.

"Well, even if I was hypnotized, why would Jack tell me to break things just because somebody said a certain word?" Tycho wondered.

"Like . . . *window?*" Vicky suggested experimentally.

While Vicky cleaned up Tycho's bowl of ice cream and chocolate sauce, Mom got on the phone. Jack's mother drove him over right away.

"But this is fantastic!" she said.

"It's not fantastic at all. It's called post-hypnotic suggestion," Dad told her.

"Well, I'm sorry," she said. "I hope Jack can undo it. It would be kind of inconvenient never to be able to say *win—*"

"Stop!" Danny shouted.

But it was too late. "*—dow,*" she had already finished.

This time it was the beautiful ceramic ashtray my college roommate had given Mom that was closest to Tycho's reach. Jack's mother swept up the pieces while the three boys made their way up to Danny's room.

But now Tycho chose to be obstinate. "I don't *want* to be hypnotized anymore," he grumbled, pouting. "What if you make me drink toilet water again?"

"Shut up, Tycho! You're going to be hypnotized, period!" Danny ordered, lunging at him with raised fists.

Jack took one step, planting himself stolidly between Danny and Tycho, fixing Danny with his calm gaze. Danny growled, but he backed off.

Jack remained rooted in place, thinking for a long moment. "Uh . . . wait outside, Danny," he finally said, in his usual measured tones.

"You don't need me to hold the flashlight?" Danny objected.

"I can manage," Jack said. "We'll both be in trouble if Tycho doesn't stop. It won't take long. And then . . . then I'll tell you a secret."

"But I don't want to be hynotized," Tycho protested again. It was strange; you'd think he would have been *eager* to stop helplessly breaking things.

"It'll be worth it, Tycho, I promise," Jack assured him. "You'll see. We'll be out soon, Danny."

Danny was too impatient to stand there doing nothing while he waited out in the hall—and even at that age, he loved to invent experiments. He thought for a minute, then quickly placed a chair just outside the closed door of his room. He put Tycho's prized Mickey Mouse alarm clock on the chair, making sure it was the only object that would be within Tycho's immediate reach when he came out of the room.

A few minutes later, Tycho and Jack emerged into the upstairs hall. "Window!" Danny instantly shouted.

"What are you talking about?" Tycho asked him. "And what's my clock doing here?" He picked it up carefully and took it back to his own room.

"You want to hear that secret, Danny?" Jack asked him, beckoning him back into the hypnosis chamber. They were in there for about ten minutes.

It was just around this time that Danny began to stop picking on Tycho. We all assumed that Danny's abuse of Tycho came to an end simply because Tycho was getting to be Danny's size.

But I thought I noticed, on a couple of occasions, Tycho uttering the word *door* just when Danny was about to attack him. And, oddly enough, as soon as Danny heard the word, he would stiffly turn away and leave Tycho alone.

The Séance

The houses in our middle-class neighborhood were all set well back from the street. Most of the other people on the block, concerned with appearances, concentrated their gardening energies on the front lawns, to impress the neighbors. But Dad didn't care much about the front yard, where we never spent any time. He worked harder on the backyard lawn, which our family could enjoy in privacy. And so when we wanted to run around under the sprinkler, which created mudholes in the grass, we did it in front, where it didn't matter because only the neighbors could see it.

We did have a sort of playground in the backyard, a paved area where there had once been a garage. On the left was a great mound of sand, where we made miniature cities and used the hose to create lakes and rivers.

The neighborhood cats and dogs loved the sand, too, but for a different reason. Once Dad's boss and his wife came to dinner, and the wife, a sweet elderly lady, said gushingly to Vicky and me, "Oh, what a lovely sand pile you two children have to play in!"

"That's not a sand pile," said Vicky, who was five. "It's a shit pit."

Next to the shit pit was a 500-gallon army water-storage tank, which was our swimming pool. It was a hideously ugly round black rubber container about ten feet in diameter and three feet high. You couldn't exactly swim laps in it, but we weren't into swimming laps; we were into cooling off in the hot summers, splashing each other, doing underwater somersaults, and skinny-dipping with our friends when our parents weren't home. The water froze in the winter. Before sliding around on it ourselves, Vicky and I would plop Danny or Tycho down on the ice first, to see if it was strong enough. In spring we would watch with fascination the thousands of mosquito larvae floating just below the surface, breathing through their tiny probosciscs, soon to leave this ideal breeding ground and take over the neighborhood.

There was nothing in the large space to the right of the swimming pool until the day before Vicky's sixth

birthday, when she found Dad's present to her there—
a pile of lumber. He was going to build her a playhouse,
he told her, the best playhouse in the world. "Oh, how
wonderful! Can I have my party in it tomorrow?" she
naively asked him. He cautioned her that it might not
be finished by then.

Eight years later, he had completed the foundation,
the floor, and three walls. It wasn't only that he was the
world's greatest procrastinator. He also did everything
with extreme thoroughness. The playhouse foundation
alone, Mom used to say, would support the Empire State
Building. Dad never finished it, but what there is of that
playhouse will probably still be standing long after the
house itself has collapsed.

Vicky never did have a birthday party in the playhouse.
Instead, it was the setting for the séance I conducted the
summer after ninth grade.

When I was in grade school, Mom had organized many
creatively weird parties for me, the best ones being Halloween parties. These parties took place in my room in
the refinished attic on the third floor. It was the perfect
setting for a Halloween party because Mom had allowed
my friends and me to paint a mural on one entire wall.
Several of us participated, but the most gruesomely effective sections had been done by my friend Nicole. She
was a shy, plump girl who was a brilliant artist. The
central figure was a rather glamorous witch standing

behind a bubbling cauldron. She was surrounded by all manner of grotesque creatures—bats, demons, imps, octopus-like things with claws.

For the Halloween parties, the rest of the house would be darkened; no one would be at the front door to greet the guests. Instead, there was a series of posters to show the guests the way up, painted by Nicole. They weren't grade-school work; they were very professional. We used the same posters at every Halloween party for years, and they are probably still somewhere in the house. The first one, posted beside the front door, showed a man hanging from a noose, obviously dead because the angle of his head indicated his neck was broken. But one of his bony hands was pointing inside the house. And written underneath in scraggly letters was the instruction: *Walk in. Follow the spooks.*

The only lights inside illuminated Nicole's other posters, located at strategic intervals to indicate the way up the creaky stairs. One showed a Frankenstein monster, holding a dead child in one hand and pointing with the other. The next was a hideously decayed corpse, rotten flesh dangling from its face as it rose from a coffin, one arm outstretched. Finally there was a leering skeleton in a moonlit graveyard, gesturing at the flight of steps up to the attic.

We did some of the conventional Halloween things, like bobbing for apples and carving pumpkins. Nicole's pumpkins were always the most unusual and the most intricately and delicately executed.

Then, with the candlelit pumpkins arranged around the room, Mom would read aloud a couple of truly hor- rifying ghost stories about haunted houses, nightmares coming true, people being followed by ghouls. Often a terrified guest or two would call their mothers to be taken home at this point, which was too bad because the best part came next—fortune-telling.

Mom wrote the fortunes before the party, typing them on little pieces of paper, and folded them up and placed them in a bowl. Each kid would pick one and read it, and they were all horrible—things like: *You will work hard for many, many years and finally earn a million dollars—and then it will all be stolen from you by your children, and you will die penniless.* Or *You will develop an incurable neurological disorder and spend the rest of your life as a gibbering idiot in an insane asylum.* The best fortune, every year, was *I'm sorry, my dear, but you have no future. . . .* I remember when Nicole got that one. She just smiled and carefully folded it up and kept it.

Naturally, these Halloween parties were a big hit with the kids in fifth and sixth grade, and that meant I was (conditionally, at least) accepted by all. In elementary school, it wasn't social death to be associated with some- one, like me, who was a little different.

But things changed in junior high. Suddenly we were surrounded by older kids, teenagers, who had very rigid rules of dress and speech, which were hopelessly confusing to me. Before we became deliberate nonconformists in high school, Vicky had been on the verge of being accepted by the popular kids in junior high. I, on the other hand, never had a chance with those people; I never had the right clothes, I was lousy at sports, I couldn't catch on to the slang, and the tuft of hair on the back of my head wouldn't lie flat. I was always an oddball, a nothing in the eyes of the ruling clique.

I'll never forget the time in seventh grade when I was just getting to be friends with a guy named Dave Solomon. He lived in another neighborhood but one day rode home with me on the school bus. A popular kid named Steve Kamen asked Dave what he was doing on this bus. "I'm going over to Bill's house," Dave explained. Kamen looked at me, then back to Dave. "You sap," he told Dave, and walked away.

But despite Steve Kamen's disapproval, Dave became my good friend in junior high. Like me, Dave played the piano and was more interested in music and literature than in sports. Unlike me, Dave had a chance to be popular at the beginning of seventh grade—he was naturally better at sports than I was, despite his lack of interest, and at the start of the year a lot of the girls considered him to be very cute. That changed when he was suddenly struck by virulent acne, which persisted throughout his teenage years and left him with scars that were not merely physical.

I had other friends in junior high, too. We were an extremely disparate group but had certain traits in common that made us comfortable together; we read a lot, we liked being smart, we didn't fit in with the conventional kids—and gradually began to realize that we didn't *want* to fit in with them.

My best friend was still Nicole, who had painted the Halloween posters. She was now a tall, overweight girl, who was generally recognized as the smartest person in the school. In eighth grade, we had an English teacher who was new to the school, and he gave Nicole an F on her first paper. Nicole, in her quiet, self-effacing way, did not protest or even ask the teacher why he had given her the F, as I urged her to do when she told me about it over the phone. "It doesn't really matter," she said, no particular emotion in her voice, as though she accepted such injustice as a normal part of life.

A few days later, the same teacher had us write an essay in class. When he saw what Nicole came up with, in front of his eyes, he apologized to her privately for giving her the F on her first paper, explaining that it was so well written he had assumed she had copied it word for word from a published article. He changed the original grade, and his opinion of Nicole.

Though Nicole always got very good grades, she claimed she hardly ever studied. Mom didn't believe her—she said *nobody* could do so well without studying. But Nicole was telling the truth, all right. I knew how much of her own study time Nicole spent writing papers for other kids who were not good writers, though of course I couldn't give this evidence to Mom.

Mom also didn't believe what Nicole said about her weight problem. No one ever saw Nicole overeat, and Nicole told me that she really didn't eat much when she was alone either; she said she was overweight because there was something about her metabolism that turned every morsel of food she put into her mouth into fat. Mom said that was baloney; she was sure Nicole overate in secret. On this issue I had no evidence one way or the other—until many years later.

Nicole and I had no romantic interest in each other, but we spent a lot of time every night talking on the phone. We loved discussing the other kids, and Nicole had remarkable insight into human nature. She always seemed to understand *why* people did things—even people who were very different from herself.

Such as Matilda, who was one of our closest friends, but in many ways Nicole's direct opposite. Matilda was quite thin and ate very little in order to maintain her eighteen-inch waist. Today she would have been considered pretty, but her frizzy red hair was unfashionable in those days. (Eventually she learned the trick of ironing it.) She was taller than Nicole and stood in a slouch. Matilda adored books and read more voraciously than any of us. Her grades were even better than Nicole's— her grade-point average of 98.6 was the highest on record in the history of the school system. But unlike Nicole, Matilda's grades were the result of relentless studying. When we did *A Tale of Two Cities* in English class, Matilda read the book so many times that she could recite as much of it as anyone could stand to listen to—"It was the best of times; it was the worst of times . . ."—from memory. She studied all day on weekends and holidays. She didn't stop when she had completed all the required work; she would then write extra papers that were not even assigned by the teachers.

We all laughed when Matilda told us how her parents tried to bribe her to calm down about schoolwork by offering her twenty-five dollars if she would ever get a B in a course, fifty dollars for two B's, and so on. Matilda was witty, and the way she told the story made it seem very funny. We never found out if her parents would have kept the bargain because she went right on piling up A's in everything.

Nicole and I talked about Matilda a lot. Nicole felt that part of Matilda's problem was that she saw herself as unattractive. She had to excel at something, and that was going to be scholarship—and her eighteen-inch waist.

Bart was another close friend. Because he was regarded as the smartest boy in school, it was assumed that he and Nicole belonged together, and they did sort of go out with each other. Bart was a basically decent guy, but I always thought twice before asking his opinion about anything I had done; he seemed to enjoy expressing unpleasant truths.

I did not have a Halloween party all through junior high. But the summer after ninth grade, I hit on the idea of conducting a séance in the playhouse at the end of the backyard. It was dark out there, and the half-finished wooden building was like something from a ghost town. I planned the séance carefully, with Nicole's help. The only part Nicole didn't help me with was the actual script. I spent several days writing it myself, laughing a lot, and kept the contents a secret from Nicole. Typically, she never tried to coerce me into telling her what was in it.

But Nicole was the brains behind the recording I made on Dad's big, clunky tape recorder. Nicole created sound effects by coaxing weird noises out of various musical instruments and then making them weirder by speeding up or slowing down the tape. Nicole helped me figure out how to disguise my voice by speaking through an electric fan, which gave an effect of windy, echoing distance. But I didn't record the script until Nicole had gone home; I wanted the actual words to be a surprise for her as well as everybody else.

The day of the séance, Dad brought home a big piece of dry ice from the lab, which we kept in the freezer until the last moment. (The dry ice was Nicole's idea, too.) I carried a table out to the playhouse and, with several extension cords, set up the tape recorder under the table. I put a cauldronlike cast-iron pot on the table for the dry ice, and on one side of it I arranged a flashlight so the beam would hit my face from below. Nicole had loaned me some mascara, and I painted wrinkles on my face with it, blackened my lips, and wore a black robe Nicole had found at a junk store. Just before my friends arrived, I put the dry ice in the pot, where it began to generate wafting clouds of vapor.

I was waiting for my friends in the half-lit playhouse as they made their way down to the end of the dark backyard. The idea was that I was a medium, contacting an authority in the spirit world who knew what lay in store for each of my friends. They sat down at the creaking table and joined hands. Mist billowed around my dimly lit, lined, and demonic features. Various wavering hoots and moans floated up from under the table. I sighed and groaned awhile myself and then announced, "The contact is there, I can feel it coming, it's taking over me, it's . . ." My head lolled forward.

I had seated my friends around the table in the same order as their futures were related on the tape. "And what lies in store for Matilda, Master?" I said dully, as though speaking in a trance. Tall, thin Matilda, with her unfashionably kinky red hair, who spent about 90 percent of her waking hours with a book and already knew more about literature than most of our teachers, was sitting just beside me.

"For Matilda . . . Ah, yes, fame and glamour lie in store for this fortunate creature," intoned the tape. "She will marry an illiterate and gluttonous multimillionaire, and the two of them will spend the rest of their lives watching soap operas on TV and devouring candy. By the age of thirty, she will be as grotesquely obese as her husband."

"Perfect!" Matilda crowed, laughing just as hard as the others.

"For poor Dave, the future is not so bright," predicted the voice. "His sheer lack of talent will make him a failure at all 'serious' musical pursuits. He will become a poorly paid salesman at a flea-bitten record store catering to the tastes of moronic adolescents. He will spend his days listening to the raucous blare of popular idols and at an early age will grow deafened by the sounds and end his life in poverty."

Dave wasn't so thrilled by this—he and I were intensely competitive. He grunted and muttered, "Thanks a lot, Bill." Everyone else was chuckling, though.

Bart and Nicole—two of the most brilliant kids in the school—came last; their prediction created the most satisfying reaction of all. "Ah, for these two the future is so hideous that it pains even me to utter it," droned the voice. "For them, only thankless, unceasing toil and drudgery lie in store. Due to their extreme mental incompetence, their career opportunities will be limited indeed. They will spend the rest of their lives cleaning the toilets at Westgate Junior High. . . ."

By this point, not only Bart but almost all the others were happily hooting and guffawing. I glanced over at Nicole. Of course, she wasn't insulted by her future, as Dave had been. No one could take this particular prediction seriously. But there was something about Nicole's smile that indicated cleaning toilets was exactly the kind of thing she had known I would come up with for her all along.

It would be cute if I could now surprise the reader by saying that these predictions unexpectedly came true. But of course, they were intended to be farcical and ironic, the most highly unlikely futures I could come up with for everyone. Naturally, Matilda became an erudite professor and an author, not an obese TV addict. Bart is a successful scientist, not a cleaner of toilets. And though Dave dropped in and out of college for awhile and had various jobs, he never worked in a record store and is now seriously studying musical composition.

Nicole spent part of her high school senior year as a foreign exchange student in Italy. Previously an atheist, like many of my friends, in Italy she had a deep religious experience, a calling. She lost a lot of weight. And after college, to Matilda's horror, Nicole entered an order of nuns.

It is not a teaching order, as one would have expected of brilliant Nicole, but a more radical group. Though not missionaries, the sisters in her order live with the poor, in the same housing conditions, some in the bleakest projects in the United States, others in the most poverty-stricken developing countries. They support themselves by doing the same kind of menial work as the people they live with. . . .

Nicole, the smartest person I ever knew, has spent much of her life working in factories, operating steam-pressing machines in non–air-conditioned industrial laundries in the tropics, giving bed baths in inner-city hospitals—and cleaning toilets.

Of all my childhood friends, she is the happiest and the most genuinely satisfied with her life.

The Pitiful Encounter

As teenagers, Vicky and I talked a lot about hating people. At the dinner table, we would go on and on about all the popular kids we hated at high school. Dad, who has a very logical mind, sometimes cautioned us about this. "Don't waste your hate on them," he would say. "Save it up for important people, like the president." We responded by quoting the famous line from *Medea:* "Loathing is endless. Hate is a bottomless cup; I pour and pour."

What Dad did not understand was that hate was not exactly what we were talking about. We had something a little different in mind; that was why Vicky and her two best friends, Avis and Eleanor, had coined their special term, *pituh*. There was no word in the English language that specified all the particular characteristics that made someone pituh. Though it was pronounced something like the first two syllables of *pitiful*, the term certainly did not mean that the person was pitiful or pathetic in the sense of being an outcast. On the contrary, most of the people our group considered to be pituh were members of the popular clique: the girls with perfectly groomed beehive hairdos who giggled and flirted and were always fixing their makeup; the arrogant guys they flirted with, athletic types who rarely opened a book and who considered me a nonentity because I was lousy at sports. It was these slaves to peer pressure whom we considered the most pituh of all—somehow they did not seem to understand that we, as oddballs and deliberate nonconformists, were far superior to them in every way.

We were the first hippies at our high school. We wore ancient sandals, carried our books in cloth sacks, and let our hair grow long and untamed. Vicky and Avis were the most daring. They pried discarded gum out of the school drinking fountains and casually popped it into their mouths to chew—making sure, of course, that pituh-people were observing them. The resulting expressions of bafflement and awed disgust were a joy to behold. Vicky and Avis insisted they weren't just doing this for effect. They claimed that ABC gum ("Already Been

Chewed") had a far more subtle depth of character than the unripened fresh stuff.

The pituh-people at school were not the only ones we took pleasure in bewildering. There was also the general public. Avis had spent a year in England when her father was on sabbatical there and had returned with the ability to speak, when she chose, in a gratingly intense Cockney accent. " 'Ave yuh gawt inny boiros?" she demanded of drugstore clerks, who had no idea she was asking for a ball-point pen. But the best use of her accent was a game we called The Pitiful Encounter, which the three girls played frequently on streetcars.

In order to explain The Pitiful Encounter, it is necessary to point out that Avis was not as attractive as the other two. She was not unpretty, but she was overweight, with a fleshy face and mousy hair. Physically lazy, she carried herself with a slump. Eleanor, in contrast, was tall, thin, delicately featured. There was an elfin quality about her. And Vicky was a real beauty, earthier than Eleanor, with huge blue eyes, prominent dimples, and thick strawberry blonde hair. Her looks were so stunning that, had she not consciously chosen otherwise, she could have been a member of the popular pituh-group at school.

On the day The Pitiful Encounter was born, the four of us had gone shopping downtown on a Saturday and were waiting for the streetcar home. Vicky and Eleanor and I—for some reason I now forget—looked almost like normal people, in clothes that actually matched, our hair neatly groomed. Vicky and Eleanor were even wearing makeup, in which they would never have been caught dead at school. Avis was dressed in one of her typical outfits—a discarded mud-brown sweater of her father's, moth-eaten and far too big, which emphasized her plumpness. It looked particularly hideous with an olive green skirt she had found at a thrift store, frayed at the hem and unfashionably long, which she wore with thick black knee socks. As usual, her hair was a mess, falling into her eyes.

Vicky and Eleanor and I boarded the streetcar first and took a long seat together. The only other empty seat was two rows ahead of us. Avis, who was not timid, asked the icily prim-looking woman sitting in a single seat directly across the aisle from us if she would mind moving so that Avis could sit with her friends. The woman sighed irritably but began gathering her parcels together.

And then Vicky, aware of how outrageously dowdy and bedraggled Avis looked in contrast to us, was struck by sudden inspiration. "Don't bother moving," she told the woman. "*We* don't want to sit anywhere near *her.*"

The woman frowned, rolled her eyes, and sank back into her seat, shaking her head.

Avis was momentarily nonplussed. Then, responding

to Vicky's subtle but significant nod, she caught on. "But I thought we might, yer know, 'ave a little chat," she said to us with a sad, hopeful smile, laying on her Cockney accent.

"Go away!" Vicky said, loudly enough for the other passengers to hear. "You can't sit with us!"

"But I jist want t'be yer friend," Avis faltered.

The woman Avis had asked to move was looking back and forth between them. The other passengers had fallen silent, listening. I was a little embarrassed, but not Vicky. "Well, you *can't* be our friend! You talk funny. We don't like you!" Vicky savagely retorted.

"Just leave us alone," Eleanor added, finally getting the idea.

Avis cringed away and took the seat two rows ahead.

"Can you believe she actually thought we would let her *sit* with us?" Vicky asked us, bristling with indignation, her voice clearly audible throughout the car.

Avis sank lower in her seat, staring straight ahead, wiping her eyes.

The unfriendly woman who Avis had asked to move got up and walked over to her. "Just ignore those nasty kids," she said gently. "You're a better person than they are. Remember that."

Avis struggled to suppress her giggles, to press her lips together and maintain her miserable demeanor in front of the now kindly woman and the other outraged passengers. Only when we got off the streetcar could she let it out, explosively, as the girls clung to each other, bent over in mirth.

That was the only time I played The Pitiful Encounter; somehow, the reactions of the other passengers made me too self-conscious to get a kick out of it. But the three girls loved it. The game worked even better the next time they played it: An old man gave Avis a dollar and on his way out told Vicky and Eleanor they should be ashamed of themselves. Another time, a woman with a little girl comforted Avis and told her child she hoped she would *never* grow up to be like those horrible girls. Such responses were irresistibly entertaining to Vicky and her two friends. They rode the streetcar now with no destination in mind, continuing to play The Pitiful Encounter. They practiced and honed it—though it often required an almost superhuman effort on Avis's part not to ruin it all by bursting into laughter in front of some compassionate stranger.

But on one memorable occasion, The Pitiful Encounter had unexpected consequences, as they described to me in detail.

Avis was sitting by herself in a double seat, across the aisle and one row behind Vicky and Eleanor. The other passengers didn't seem to be noticing them that day— no kindly person stepped forward at the usual moment. Perhaps their role-playing had grown routine after so many performances. To get things moving, Vicky and Eleanor had no choice but to become more brutal, adding special twists to their usual insults.

"You'd think she'd at least go on a diet," Vicky said. "And all those hideously disgusting pimples! You think she ever washes her face?"

"She doesn't take too many baths or brush her teeth too often, *that's* for sure," Eleanor said, wrinkling her nose and fanning the air in front of her.

"And the way she talks is so *stupid!*" Vicky said vehemently. "She should learn that *we* don't talk that way in America."

"Can't 'elp the wy I tawk," Avis mumbled, her lip quivering.

Vicky rolled her eyes in a brilliant imitation of pituh-behavior. "How can somebody so pathetic even stand to *exist?*" she asked, shaking her head in wonder.

"You have a very charming accent. Where do you come from?" said a male voice.

Vicky and Eleanor spun around. Because of the lack of response, they were farther along the streetcar line than usual now, where the tracks passed the university. None of them had noticed the three boys who had gotten on at the university stop. But now the boys were standing in the aisle, and one of them had his hand on the back of Avis's seat.

Avis hesitated. Nothing like this had ever happened

before. All three of the boys were extremely good-looking and not the least bit pituh—especially the one leaning over her with his hand on the back of her seat.

"Um, I'm from, uh, London, England," Avis finally said.

"That's very interesting. Do you mind if we join you?"

"Er, uh, no," Avis said, fighting the impulse to glance over at Vicky and Eleanor.

The especially good-looking boy slid in beside her; the other two took the seat behind. Vicky nudged Eleanor, who was openly staring at them. Eleanor quickly turned back; the two of them did their best to look straight ahead and pretend indifference—to listen to, and not watch, what was happening to Avis.

"You must be pretty sophisticated, coming from a cosmopolitan city like London," the boy was saying. "How long have you been here?"

"Since, uh, the beginning of term," Avis improvised.

"Funny we haven't noticed you around campus before," another of the boys said.

"Oh, I ain't at university yet," Avis said in her richest Cockney, finally beginning to relax and enjoy herself. "I'm in 'igh school."

"You seem much more mature than that," the third boy said. "Probably because you've traveled so much."

Vicky and Eleanor glanced at each other, not smiling.

This was getting a little tough to take—these were college boys!

"You must find the attitudes around here pretty provincial," the boy beside Avis said. "Especially among high school students. Those little kids can be pretty narrow-minded—and too ignorant to know it."

"You should really be hanging out with people more on your own level," another boy said.

"Vicky, what are we going to do?" Eleanor whispered.

"I don't *know!*" Vicky muttered grimly.

"Listen, uh . . . What's your name?" the boy beside Avis said.

"Avis."

"Hi. I'm Art, and this is Bob and Gary. I think Bob's right; you're wasting your time with those high school children." He looked up at his friends. "What do you think? About Friday night, I mean."

"Great idea," Bob said.

"Friday night?" Avis asked, unable to control her curiosity.

"We're having a party on Friday night," Art told her. "Why don't you come? I mean, if your parents wouldn't mind. We'd like to get to know you better. And you'd meet lots of interesting people."

"We'll make sure you have a great time," Gary added encouragingly.

"Come on, Eleanor," Vicky said, standing up with determination. "Enough is enough." They moved across the swaying streetcar aisle. Vicky smiled charmingly at the boys. "Hi," she said. "I'm Vicky, and this is Eleanor. We're really Avis's friends."

The boys turned reluctantly away from Avis and regarded Vicky and Eleanor with silent hostility.

Vicky brandished her dimples. "Uh, you know, that was just a game," she explained. "Avis really *is* our best friend. Right, Avis?"

Avis said nothing.

Eleanor pushed back her long, white blonde hair. "We do this all the time, just kind of for laughs," she said. "We're all in it together, aren't we, Avis?"

Again, Avis said nothing.

"For laughs, huh?" Bob said, not sounding at all amused.

"Pretty juvenile sense of humor," Art remarked.

"It's a sign of deep insecurity, putting another person down to try to feel good about yourselves," Gary pointed out.

"Anyway, we were in the middle of a conversation," said Art, the gorgeous one beside Avis. "Would you mind letting us continue it?"

"Avis, *tell them!*" Vicky insisted.

"Tell them what?" Avis asked her, sounding completely innocent. "That you two walk around with yer noses in the air, treatin' me as if I was dirt? And then these three young men start treatin' me like a 'uman bein', and suddenly yer all cozy and sweetsy?" She folded her arms across her chest.

"*Avis!*" Vicky cried out in furious, powerless frustration. "The game is over! Stop it! Just tell them the *truth!*"

Art sighed, giving Vicky a disgusted look, and turned back to Avis, who smiled sweetly at him. "This is our stop," he said. He tore a page out of his notebook and wrote on it. "Here's our address and phone number. Call us if you need a lift on Friday."

The three boys got up, brushing rudely past Vicky and Eleanor. "Bye, Avis. See you on Friday," they said, grinning engagingly at her, and dismounted the streetcar with casual college-boy aplomb.

Now Avis was the only one laughing. "I just couldn't *resist,*" she gasped, barely able to get the words out. "I mean . . . when . . . when would another opportunity like that ever come along?"

"Avis, we are *never* going to forgive you," Vicky said, fuming. "Will we, Eleanor?"

"Never," Eleanor agreed. "What's their address, Avis?"

Leah's Stories

When I was in high school, I got to know a strange, smart girl named Leah Moses. She had coarse black hair, an oily complexion, and thick glasses. Though she had independently styled her appearance like the girls in our group—long hair, no makeup—she was never accepted as a member of our circle. Most of our friends couldn't stand her because she was such a pretentious intellectual snob.

Bart and Nicole and I were the only ones who ever spent any time with Leah at all. Partly, the three of us felt sorry for her. Leah was truly an outcast, not one by choice, like Vicky. Nor were her shabby clothes an affectation, as ours were: Leah's family was poor; she could not afford to dress any other way. But we didn't associate with her only out of pity; we were entertained by the outrageous things she said.

Leah claimed she had a serious and physically intimate relationship with a wealthy and titled English athlete–scholar named Neville Asquith-Smythe. She was always telling us how handsome and well built Neville was. He was a brilliant college philosophy major. Leah often attended classes with him at the university, and she went on at length about his explanations of Hegel and Kant. But she was never able to produce Neville. When I mentioned him to a friend of my parents who was a philosophy professor, he said there was no English philosophy major at the university.

Leah bragged a lot about her older sister Ze'eva (she never neglected to pronounce the apostrophe), who had been three years ahead of us in high school, was recognized by all as the most brilliant and beautiful student in her class, and now lived on a kibbutz in Israel and fought in the Israeli army. Beginning to be suspicious, I asked Vera Greenberg, who had been in that class, about Leah's sister. She said nobody named Ze'eva Moses had been in her class, or in any classes for several years before or after hers, and proved it by showing me her yearbooks.

On the few occasions when Bart and Nicole and I invited Leah to do something with us on a Friday evening, she always refused. Leah said she was a member of an advanced folk-dancing group that practiced on Fridays and often performed in public. She couldn't miss a single rehearsal. The director of the group, she told us, was an exceptionally attractive man in his twenties named Russell Davidson, who was independently wealthy because his family owned the Davidson Brothers chemical company. Russ, as Leah called him, was married, but he was always making passes at her anyway when he picked her up in his Rolls-Royce Silver Cloud. Of course, he never picked her up in his Rolls-Royce at school, or anyplace else where we might actually lay eyes on it.

Nicole, whose opinions about people I always trusted, said that Leah was a pathological liar. But she wouldn't let Bart confront her with our proof. She pointed out that to do so would have been cruel and—even worse— embarrassing. It might have been different if Leah's stories were destructive to others; in fact, the only person they hurt was Leah herself.

But once, after we'd been hearing about folk dancing and Russ and his Rolls-Royce for several months, Bart couldn't resist saying, "Gee, this Friday folk-dancing thing sounds like fun. You think we could ever come, too?"

"I doubt it," Leah said with predictable haste. "It *is* a very exclusive and professional group. They're extremely selective about who they allow to participate; they have to be."

Privately, the three of us wondered what Leah *really* did on Friday evenings. If she didn't stay at home alone, we figured she was probably forced by her elderly parents to attend religious services or visit even more elderly relatives.

But two weeks after Bart had asked Leah if we could go to folk dancing, Leah phoned me on Friday afternoon to say that Russ had generously granted her permission to invite three of her more mature and sophisticated friends that night—just this once, of course—and she felt Bart and Nicole and I were the only ones who would prove acceptable.

I was very surprised that Leah had invited us; she had never suggested introducing us to her nonexistent boyfriend or showed us photographs of her imaginary sister. Why would Leah volunteer to expose her lies and humiliate herself in this case? I told her I'd think about it, hung up, and called Nicole and Bart, who were both at Nicole's house.

Nicole's interpretation was that Leah probably knew we were going to a party that night to which she had not been invited. Asking us to her imaginary folk-dancing group was safe, since she certainly did not expect us to skip the party to go with her. Leah's phone call was nothing but a feeble attempt to improve her credibility.

"What do you think she'd do if we *did* agree to go?" I wondered.

"It might be interesting to see what kind of excuse she'd come up with," Bart said. "Why don't you tell her we accept?"

I was reluctant to put Leah on the spot, but I was also curious. And it wouldn't be so embarrassing to do this to her over the phone. I called Leah back and nodded knowingly to myself when she said that unfortunately Russ was not picking her up in his Rolls that night, after all. It was so irritatingly predictable that I couldn't keep from saying, "So you weren't really inviting us?"

There was a long silence on the other end of the phone, as I expected. But I was not prepared when Leah asked if one of us could get a car tonight. She didn't have access to a car, but she knew the way. I said sure and slowly hung up, wishing I hadn't accepted. We would miss the party. And probably all that would happen was that Leah would pretend to get lost, and we'd just drive around aimlessly, listening to more of her stories. Nicole and Bart felt the same way. But it was too late to back out now.

We didn't get lost; Leah gave Bart excellent directions. We could hardly believe it when she pointed out an old warehouse downtown and told him to park at the next space he could find. As we walked back toward the building, there was no need for her to draw our attention to

the gigantic and gleaming Rolls-Royce Silver Cloud re-
posing majestically in front of the shabby, unlit doorway.
No one could *not* have noticed that car. We exchanged
glances of amazement. None of us had ever seen a ve-
hicle like that in our lives.

Lively ethnic music in a minor key grew louder as we
climbed the four dingy flights of metal stairs. Leah
pushed open a door on a landing lit by an unadorned
light bulb and stepped inside. We shyly followed her into
a large room with bare walls and a scuffed wooden floor.
Unfamiliar instruments tooted and trilled rhythmically
from a phonograph equipped with two large, expensive-
looking speakers.

A group of about a dozen people, college age and older,
danced in a line holding hands. The women had long
hair and no makeup and wore bright peasant skirts and
blouses. Many of the men had beards, and all wore jeans
and T-shirts—except one, who stood out from the rest
in black trousers and turtleneck. He was tall and very
lean, with short hair and no beard or mustache, and he
danced at the head of the line, leading the others along.

Their feet moved in complicated patterns, hopping oc-
casionally, jumping back and then forward again, as the
line snaked around the room. Sometimes the leader
would lower his head and glide underneath two other
dancers' joined hands, pulling the line around and

through itself. Everyone was sweating and smiling. The leader never missed a beat, one arm held above his head, his face lifted almost ecstatically as his feet breezed through the intricate steps. Some of the others, I was relieved to see, stumbled at times, losing count, looking down at their feet, their mouths moving silently as though repeating instructions. They were too involved to pay any attention to our arrival. Leah ran out onto the floor, grabbed the hand of the person at the end of the line, and plunged skillfully into the dance—though she wasn't particularly graceful.

When the music ended, they all dropped hands and began talking and laughing, wiping their brows and catching their breath. Leah introduced us to Russ, the leader, and his wife, Maria.

Russ wasn't nearly as handsome as Leah had described him, but he was good-looking enough, with a narrow face and a long jaw. He didn't say much; he was clearly eager to get on with the next dance and hurried back to the phonograph. Maria, who had thin brown hair and a round face and wore a knitted shawl, was very gracious. She said in a gentle voice that she was glad to meet Leah's friends and was happy we had come and that it was really easier than it looked and she hoped we'd have a good time.

"Do *Mayim* next, Russ," she called over to him. "That's

the best one to get people started on. It's an Israeli dance about water," she said quietly again to us. "You'll catch on right away. Come on."

Though we were awkward and self-conscious at first, *Mayim* did turn out to be pretty easy. You did a few simple steps around in a circle, then ran into the center and back with your arms raised during the chorus, chanting *"Mayim"* along with the singers on the record. We felt breathless and invigorated when it was over and even more invigorated at the end of the evening, after stumbling through, and eventually learning, more complex dances.

"Please come back," Maria said, as though she meant it, and even Russ nodded encouragingly in his inarticulate way. "Feel free to bring other friends, too—the more people, the more fun it is," Maria urged us.

It occurred to me to ask Leah why she had told us this group was so exclusive and that the leaders were reluctant for her to bring anybody, when in fact they were clearly eager for more participants. But I was in such high spirits that I didn't feel like pinning Leah down—especially because she did not seem to share our ebullience, but was strangely distant on the way home.

Vicky was intrigued when I told her how much fun folk dancing had been and described to her the seemingly far-out, counter-cultural people who had been there—

not to mention the incredible Rolls-Royce. Vicky was also somewhat incredulous that dumpy *Leah,* who pathetically invented all those stories about herself, would actually be involved in anything so interesting. But she was free the next Friday and decided to give it a try. She asked Avis and Eleanor to come, too, as insurance in case it *did* turn out to be boring. I invited Dave, and Nicole asked Matilda to come.

It didn't occur to me to mention any of this to Leah, though I was thoughtful enough to ask her, at school on Friday, if she needed a ride that night.

"A ride?" she said, as though she didn't know what I meant.

"Yeah. To folk dancing."

"You're coming *back*?" she said, a funny expression on her face. "All three of you?"

"Sure. You saw what a good time we had. And Vicky and Avis and Eleanor and Dave and Matilda are coming, too."

"But . . ." Leah's eyes swam around behind her thick glasses. She didn't know what to say.

"It's okay, isn't it?" I asked her. "Maria told us to bring more people. She said the more the better."

Leah lifted her chin. "Thanks, but I don't need a ride," she said. "Russ is picking me up in the Rolls." It wasn't *his* Rolls now; it was "the Rolls."

"I know this is going to be boring," Avis kept saying grumpily all the way downtown. She stopped complaining when she saw the Rolls-Royce, parked grandly in the same spot it had occupied the week before. Since Leah wasn't with us now, we took our time examining it, peering through the smoked windows at the lush leather and teakwood interior, stroking its flanks, murmuring words of awe. It was a while before we tore ourselves away and clomped up the stairs.

Again we arrived in the middle of a dance. But this time some of the dancers—though not Leah—turned and looked when so many new and unfamiliar faces appeared at the door. Russ Davidson, I noticed, rapt though he was, glanced several times at Eleanor, who was strikingly pretty, without missing a step. And when the dance was over, he zipped right over and actually articulated an entire sentence to us, his eyes on Eleanor.

With more of our friends there, we had an even better time than we had the week before. Russ was very patient about teaching us steps to dances that the old hands already knew, focusing his attention on Eleanor, who learned quickly and was quite graceful, with her slender body and long, pale hair.

Leah made it clear, by looking the other way and tapping her plump foot, that *she* already knew these dances perfectly. She also spent more time talking to the other people there than to us. It briefly occurred to me that she must have enjoyed her unique position as the youngest member of the group—a group that had clearly accepted her, as no group of her contemporaries at school did. But I never got around to mentioning this thought to Nicole; I was too preoccupied with other people to think much about Leah.

Leah was pleasant enough to us afterward, smiling and waving when she got into the Rolls with Russ and Maria. As Russ pulled away, he looked back several times at Eleanor.

We brought more people the next week; now our friends outnumbered the others. We also began to get to know some of the original dancers; holding hands and jumping around with them broke the ice quickly. Afterward, Maria suggested going to a coffeehouse in a hip nightclub area in the city. Eleanor, Avis, and Vicky rode in the Rolls, though Leah made sure to claim the front seat. Maria was happy to ride with us.

We had fun at the coffeehouse, where there was a folk singer. Eleanor's older brother, Sid, who was taking a semester off from Harvard, borrowed the entertainer's guitar and played a few songs himself; the rest of us—except for Leah—sang along with him. Leah seemed bored by the singing, preferring to fill me in on Neville's latest theories about Wittgenstein, but Maria was very impressed with Sid's skill.

Russ sat next to Eleanor, speaking little himself but

listening closely to everything she had to say. It was flattering that these wealthy, lively, and Bohemian adults seemed to enjoy spending time with us. It became a pattern to go to the coffeehouse with the Davidsons after folk dancing. Now we couldn't wait for Friday nights.

After this had been going on for a month or so, Maria telephoned and invited Vicky and me to come to their house for dinner on Saturday—she had invited Sid and Eleanor, too. "But, uh, maybe you better not say anything about this to Leah," Maria cautioned us. We assured her we wouldn't. We were thrilled by the invitation and couldn't wait to see what their house was like.

It was not the mansion we had anticipated, but a spacious modern split-level in a subdivision. We sat in the living room before dinner; Russ played folk-dancing records. Batik prints and other folk art hung on the walls; bright woven rugs were scattered over the oak floors. The furniture was modern, the kind you'd see in expensive magazines. Unlike our parents, who furnished their houses with secondhand stuff, the Davidsons had obviously been able to buy exactly what they wanted, whatever the price.

The evening was very informal and relaxed. Maria didn't go to a lot of trouble over the food. We had overdone steaks and baked potatoes with margarine and frozen vegetables. Russ, as usual, didn't say much, but Maria was a lively conversationalist. We talked about folk music and movies and novels, and Maria asked us about our families and friends.

It was Maria who brought up the subject of Leah. "What did Leah tell you about us?" she asked casually, adjusting her shawl.

Vicky, Sid, and Eleanor turned to me. I was the only one who knew Leah very well. I wasn't sure what to say. I wanted the Davidsons to like me and find me witty, and it would be easy to put Leah down in an amusing way. But they were apparently friends with her; if I was critical of Leah, it might offend them. "She told us how much fun folk dancing was. And she did mention Russ's family business—and the Rolls-Royce."

Maria leaned forward with what seemed to be a conspiratorial smile. "Did you believe her?" she asked me in her soft, breathy voice.

It would have been an odd question—about anybody other than Leah. I remembered that Maria had specifically asked us not to tell Leah they had invited us here. Maybe I *didn't* have to be too careful, after all. "I didn't believe a word," I said.

Maria laughed. I seemed to have said the right thing. "You'd already heard all about Ze'eva, then?" she said, imitating Leah's pronunciation of the apostrophe perfectly.

I nodded. "Then I asked a friend who was in what Leah *said* was Ze'eva's high school class. She'd never heard of her—and there was no Ze'eva in any of her yearbooks."

Maria glanced at Russ, then back at me. "It's interesting that you found actual proof. We just *assumed* that Ze'eva inhabited the same world as Neville Asquith-Smythe."

"Were we ever surprised when it turned out that you two, and folk dancing and the Rolls-Royce, actually *existed*," I said.

This time Russ laughed, too. Maria shook her hair back. "Well, *we* couldn't believe it when you guys started showing up either. We were beginning to suspect that Leah had no friends at all outside that imaginary universe of hers."

"How did you get to know her?" Eleanor asked.

"She just showed up at folk dancing, almost a year ago, I guess. She found out about the group somehow. She seemed interesting—the things she told us about herself were a little more subtle at first. But then her stories got wilder, and we began to put two and two together. You have to admit, she *can* be entertaining."

There was a certain edge to Maria's voice now; I wondered if there might be any truth to Leah's remark about Russ making passes at her. But later, Maria did not seem the least bit concerned at how close Russ was sitting to Eleanor, his arm along the back of the couch, almost touching Eleanor's shoulder. On the way home, Sid mentioned that he was sure Maria had been flirting with him. If Maria had some gripe against Leah, it didn't seem to have anything to do with jealousy over her husband.

We didn't tell Leah that, more and more often, certain of us had dinner at the Davidsons' or that the Davidsons began showing up at parties of ours that Leah was not invited to. She didn't need to have it spelled out for her. It was obvious, simply from our chumminess at folk dancing, that the Davidsons had become part of a group that had never included Leah.

The Davidsons got to know our parents. Mom thought Maria was interesting and intelligent enough. She was baffled by Russ, who hardly ever said anything, and when he did, it was always about folk dancing. "All that money," Mom said, wistfully shaking her head, "and all he can think of to do with it is buy that car and run a folk dance group."

There were now so many of our cronies at folk dancing that the downtown loft room was no longer big enough. It was also inconveniently located for the majority of the participants. Russ made arrangements with a Jewish community center in our suburb, which was more attractive and a lot larger.

After the move, even more kids began to show up. The pituh-people had always gone to something called Wigwam on Friday nights, where they danced to rock music; now we oddballs had our own equivalent. It was in my junior year that folk dancing became an official high school club, with a very crowded picture in the yearbook. Leah did not come to be photographed.

It was Eleanor these days, not Leah, who was driven to folk dancing in the Rolls (as we referred to it now). Russ was fair and gave everyone a chance to experience it at one time or another; Eleanor was the constant. He even began picking us up at school; it was intensely satisfying that all the pituh-people like Steve Kamen, hanging out in front of the building, often saw us getting into that car. Leah never seemed to be around when this happened.

It was the smoothest and most silent car any of us had ever ridden in. The seats were wonderfully plush. We loved opening the teakwood bar in the backseat and pretending we were actually drinking as we floated along —though Russ, who had no interest in alcohol, never bothered to keep it stocked. He had no interest in his executive position at the chemical company either, though he dutifully appeared there and made the motions five days a week. Folk dancing was his single passion.

Leah still came to folk dancing, though she was now only a minor participant, no longer included when we went out afterward. We didn't discuss folk dancing with Leah, and she never brought it up. When Bart and Nicole and I had time to talk to her, she regaled us with increasingly elaborate stories.

We heard about her cousin, the wealthy and critically acclaimed novelist (whose books were only published in Hebrew, of course, and not available in this country). We heard how Neville had proposed to her, wanting to make her Lady Asquith-Smythe, despite his parents' objections that she was an American and a commoner. But Leah was keeping him dangling; she wasn't sure she wanted to live in England because of the climate. Anyway, she told us, she had taken advanced placement tests and had already been admitted, with large scholarships, to Radcliffe and Smith and Stanford, though she was only a junior. Once Leah disappeared for a week, telling us afterward that she had been in Israel at Ze'eva's wedding to a famous Israeli film star and director. She then mentioned that a long poem she had written had been accepted by a prestigious literary magazine and would be published at some undisclosed point in the future.

Now I was able to report these stories to Maria. Her laughter was always unusually brittle when we spoke of Leah. I did comment on this reaction to Nicole. "I think the Davidsons must have gone out of their way to be friendly to Leah at first," she said, somewhat pensively. "Like maybe they trusted her in some way, and now Maria feels insulted that Leah kept feeding her these lies. You can sort of understand it, in a way. Poor Leah."

"Leah doesn't feed them to her now," I said. "I get the feeling the Davidsons hardly ever talk to her at all anymore."

"Poor Leah," Nicole said again. She took a long time adjusting her glasses.

Naturally, no one believed Leah when she said she had decided to accept Stanford's offer and would be going to college a year early. But when the rest of us began our senior year, Leah wasn't around—though it took a while for anybody to notice. I checked with the guidance counselor, who confirmed that Leah had in fact placed out of her senior year in high school and was now at Stanford. We were all amazed—not because Leah wasn't smart enough, but because she had been telling the truth.

"Silly of her to rush things like that," Mom said. "Your high school years are important. You might as well take the time to enjoy them while you can."

There are more stories about the Davidsons and some wild parties we had, stories about Russ and Eleanor, and Maria and Sid. But they seem less important to me now than Leah's stories.

I wrote to Nicole, who was then a foreign student in Italy, about Leah's sudden departure for college. *I think she'll be happier there,* Nicole wrote back. *No wonder she wanted to get away. She had only one good thing in high school—and she lost it.*

Pituh-plays

The first true pituh-play was created and always performed by Vicky, for an audience of Danny and Tycho and me. The play's title was *Vanya, the Insane Pianist.*

Danny and Tycho were always begging Vicky to do *Vanya, the Insane Pianist,* which was funny, though (we thought) totally meaningless. None of our friends knew about Vanya, which Vicky performed only for our own family. But Vicky and I and our friends did put on other little skits at parties, which we called pituh-plays. The skits were often inspired by real people or situations or by popular movies and books.

Of course, we had always made fun of certain books.

When we were younger, we used to invent Dick-and-Jane stories, based on the elementary reading series: "See Dick. See Jane. Hear Baby Sally cry! See Jane put the knife in Baby Sally's neck. Baby Sally is very quiet now."

The telephone game was another early precursor of the pituh-play. Vicky would call a number at random (I listened on the extension), and when someone answered, she would say in a babyish voice, "Can you come to my party?"

"Who is this? Who do you want?" the stranger on the phone might say.

"It's . . . it's my birthday," the childish voice would answer. "My mommy and daddy forgot. I'm all alone. I want to have a birthday party, but I don't have any friends. Will *you* come to my party?"

Often people hung up at this point. But sometimes they fell for it. "Your mommy and daddy left you all alone? You don't have a baby-sitter?"

"All alone. And it's my *birth*day."

The voice on the other end would pause, then say something like "I'm sure your mommy and daddy really love you. I bet they're planning a surprise for you. And remember, *I* care about your birthday." One woman even sang "Happy Birthday" over the phone, as we tried to stifle our giggles.

Another of Vicky's phone gambits was to call a random

number and say, "Please help me. I'm lost. I can't find my mommy."

"You're lost? Call home."

"Nobody's home. My mommy went away on a bus and left me here."

"Call the police."

"Don't have any more money."

"But . . ." If we were lucky, the voice on the phone would start to sound really worried now. "Can you tell me where you are?"

"I'm scared," Vicky said when this happened, sounding tearful. "It's big and dirty here. There's all these buses. There's all these mean-looking men with whiskers and dirty clothes on, and they smell funny and talk funny and want to give me candy."

"Are you at the bus station? Downtown? Your mother went away on a bus and left you there?"

"Uh-huh," Vicky said, whimpering.

"Don't talk to anyone. Stay right there and I'll come and get you," the person said, then hung up. We rolled on the floor.

When Vicky grew too old to sound babyish on the phone, we began doing real pituh-plays at parties with our friends. Sometimes Vicky made up names for the characters, such as Renaissance de McCarthy or Peristalsis van Weatherbiddington. One play opened with Vicky sitting on a bench with a brown paper bag over her head and me kneeling in front of her. I was just slipping a ring onto her finger. "Yes, darling, I *will* marry you!" Vicky cried, embracing me, the paper bag crinkling against my cheek.

I sat down on the bench beside her. "Now do you think you could, maybe, uh, take the bag off?" I hesitantly suggested. "I'd love to see what you look like, just once, before we get married."

"No." She shook her head.

"But why not?"

"I'm too ugly," she said with a mournful sigh.

"You couldn't be *that* ugly. I'm sure I'll love the way you look, just like I love the way you are."

"No, you won't," she insisted. "As soon as you see how ugly I am, you'll hate me. You'll be embarrassed to be seen with me; you'll never get married to me or even stand to look at me again."

"No. I promise," I coaxed her. "I love you because you're such a wonderful person on the *inside*. It doesn't matter what you look like."

"If it doesn't matter what I look like, why do you want to see my face?"

"How can you get married to somebody and never see her face? How can I kiss you? How can I look into your eyes?"

"Well . . ." She began to soften.

"*Please,* darling," I urged her. "Do you think I'm so superficial that I'd change my mind about you because of your mere outward appearance? You know I'm not that kind of trivial person. I swear to God that I'll love and cherish you forever."

"Well . . . all right." Slowly Vicky lifted the bag from her head, her eyes squeezed shut, her shoulders hunched as though anticipating a blow.

"Why . . . you're *beautiful!*" I cried, placing my hands on her cheeks and gently turning her face toward me.

She smiled in relief. Her eyelids fluttered and lifted. She stared at me.

And then her mouth dropped open in horror. "My *God!* You're so *ugly!*" she screamed, jumping to her feet and backing away from me. "I've never seen anything so revolting in my life! What would everybody think if I got married to *that?*" She pulled the ring from her finger and hurled it at me. "I never want to see you again!" she shouted and ran from the stage.

Other pituh-plays were performed in public places. One summer evening, a group of us went to a fountain in the park, where there was always a crowd of people watching the patterns of colored lights on the falling water. Vicky had with her a small watermelon, carefully wrapped in a blanket and a frilly bonnet, no rind exposed, so that it resembled a very young baby. With the rest of us strategically placed among the crowd, Vicky cradled the baby in her arms, rocking it, murmuring to it about the pretty fountain. Bystanders smiled.

Then Vicky's voice grew louder. "You don't care about the pretty fountain, do you?" she chided the baby. "You don't care about anything but yourself. I'm getting kind of sick of that, you know?"

People were giving her funny looks. "I can't even go to the park without having to drag *you* along!" Vicky angrily accused the baby. "And your father never lifts a finger to take care of you. And all you do is make messes and scream and cry and keep me awake all night. I can't stand it anymore!" she cried, her voice becoming hysterical. "I just can't!"

People moved away from Vicky, murmuring. She stepped toward the fountain. "I can't stand it for one more second, I can't, I can't!" she screamed, lifting the baby over the water.

"No! Stop! Don't do it!" several of us shouted, running toward her.

But we were too late. With a demented shriek, Vicky hurled the baby into the shallow fountain, smashing the watermelon into a pulpy red mush. Then we got out of there, fast, before the stunned bystanders noticed the seeds.

The most elaborate pituh-play of all was Albert's brainchild. He had been reading about happenings, a new avant-garde art form. Happenings were often multimedia events in which the viewers were invited into a strange environment to interact with the artwork or the performers. In the most effective of them, Albert said, unexpected things actually *happened* to the surprised audience.

Vicky and I and many of our friends now took piano lessons from Alex Minkoff, one of the most highly regarded piano teachers in the city, whose studio was in our neighborhood. Mr. Minkoff, by his example, encouraged his students to rock back and forth while performing at recitals. He was rotund, and there was a rumor that he had once actually fallen off the piano stool in the middle of a concert.

It was Albert's idea that the happening should take the form of a recital of some of Mr. Minkoff's pupils, to which an unsuspecting audience of adults and peers would be invited. Mr. Minkoff, who had a great sense of humor, agreed enthusiastically to Albert's plan. The only restriction he imposed was to ask us not to invite any members of the professional musical community, which was fine with us—we weren't interested in shocking them. Four students were willing to perform pieces they had been working on with Mr. Minkoff. We mimeographed invitations and mailed them to several dozen people. Then we practiced—and made other detailed preparations, in and around Mr. Minkoff's studio.

On the day of the concert, one of the performers was

too sick to play. We had no choice but to go ahead without him.

The audience arrived at what appeared to be a perfectly normal concert. Mr. Minkoff often did have recitals in his studio, and the chairs were set up facing the large grand piano just as usual. The friends, parents, other adults, and the few teachers in the audience were all nicely dressed and chatted quietly as they looked over their programs before the show.

Albert performed first, a sad little Chopin étude. The music sounded more poignant than usual tonight, since the piano was noticeably out of tune.

Next, a boy named Richard played a Beethoven sonata. The famous second movement was quiet and pensive. At the most moving and beautiful moment in the piece, Richard, in his best Minkoff style, was bent over the keyboard, hardly breathing, delicately articulating the sour notes.

The apartment buzzer bleated. People jerked in their seats, then turned to frown at the door. Vera Greenberg, as planned, clicked into the room on her four-inch heels and headed for a seat near the front, right in the middle of a long row of people. "I beg your pardon," she kept repeating loudly as she squeezed past them, cracking her gum.

There was a lot of exasperated conversation during the interval before the next piece. People muttered irritably and looked over their shoulders at Vera and then at Mr. Minkoff.

I performed a Brahms intermezzo. I played on as though nothing were the matter when the grinding noises gradually began to emanate from the front of the room. (We had hidden the tape recorder behind a closed, floor-to-ceiling window curtain near the piano.) Soon the inexplicable wavering groans from the hidden tape recorder were clearly audible to everyone. Many people in the audience exchanged puzzled looks. I finished to scattered, tentative applause.

And then Vicky unexpectedly stood up. We were about to witness the first public performance of *Vanya, the Insane Pianist.*

Vicky sedately approached the piano, bowed demurely, and began to play a Chopin prelude. At first, her demeanor was very controlled. She sat bolt upright, her expression serious and withdrawn, her body motionless except for her fingers, tinkling daintily on the keys.

But as the music grew more turbulent, her torso began to sway. Her head dipped toward the keyboard, then lifted; her back arched, her chin raised, her eyes closed. She tossed her head, her long hair swinging more and more wildly, falling over her eyes. She began to moan. The music increased in volume. Now she was making glaring mistakes. The audience, suddenly dead quiet, watched Vicky in horrified astonishment. Her groans became wails; she convulsed on the bench, her open hands crashing with random violence on the keyboard. Finally she leapt to her feet in a disheveled frenzy and ran shrieking from the studio.

There was a long moment of utter, stunned silence. Then a confused, disorderly babble broke out. By now, most of the audience had finally realized that the whole thing was a joke. It was a telling test of character to see which people appreciated the humor of it (Mom and Dad were among the few who did) and which ones were highly offended.

For some reason, we stopped doing pituh-plays soon after this, moving on to more harmless pursuits, such as crashing suburban swimming pools late at night. Still, sometimes Vicky can be persuaded, even now, to do *Vanya, the Insane Pianist,* to the great amusement of her own children.

Dad's Cool

Would you like me to show you a dead body sometime?" Dad asked Vicky once when she was six. Vicky clasped her hands, breathing hard. "More than anything else in the *world!*" she cried.

Dad actually didn't show Vicky a whole dead body until years later, but we saw many other delightful things at his lab. The dreary old building where he worked at the university medical school was one of our favorite places. The large, ancient elevator had no walls, only a wire cage through which you could see the dusty cables creaking past as you rode up into the gloom. Invariably Dad scared us by jumping up and down in the elevator; the contraption would rattle and shake alarmingly. He also liked

113

to scare us in the laboratory cold room, a freezer the size of a small kitchen, where chemicals and dry ice and often interesting portions of dead animals were kept. While we were examining them, Dad would suddenly step outside and slam the heavy metal door, which could not be opened from the inside. We never knew how long he'd leave us locked up in there, shivering happily.

One of the other scientists on the same floor kept several large boa constrictors in cages in his lab. It was a treat for us to watch the snake stretch its jaws at an impossible angle to swallow a whole egg—and then day by day observe the slow progress of the egg down through the snake's sleeping body.

Even more wonderful was to be there when live mice were put into the cage. We would watch enthralled as the three mice sat on a dead tree limb, seemingly unaware of the snake's silent, gradual approach. Then, so quickly we could barely see it happening, one of the mice would be wrapped in the boa's skillful, deadly embrace. The jaws would gape and the mouse would be gone. The remaining mice never seemed to be troubled by this; they would just go on sitting there on the limb as though nothing were the matter. Their apparent dopey placidity only increased our excitement as the boa's graceful upper body moved languidly toward them again. Soon the snake's body had mouse-sized bulges in three places.

We never visited Dad's lab without begging him to

breathe helium. He usually obliged, inhaling the gas from a large metal cylinder. Helium has a peculiar effect on the vocal cords, making them vibrate more quickly than they do in an atmosphere of oxygen. When Dad started to speak after inhaling the gas, he sounded exactly like Donald Duck, and our delighted shrieks of laughter would echo down the long, dim corridor.

Once at Dad's lab, Danny, who was prodigiously mechanical but had problems learning to read, deciphered the word *pull* on a red object on the wall and followed this instruction, setting off the fire alarm. Dad handled the resulting uproar with unruffled efficiency. He was not the least bit angry; more than anything else, he was gratified by this indication that Danny might turn out to be literate, after all.

Dad always remained amazingly calm and logical in situations that would drive any other parent (even Mom) into a frenzy. "Don't get your shirt in a knot," he admonished Mom when she got upset about something he considered to be trivial. He never lost his cool—or at least almost never.

One summer afternoon when I was thirteen, my friend Angela and I arrived at the lab with a bag of balloons. We went to the sixth floor of the new addition (Dad was working in the old building), where there was a water fountain next to a balcony directly above the main entrance. We filled a balloon with water, leaned over the balcony, and waited until someone was just walking into the building. Then we let the balloon fall. It wasn't a direct hit, but close enough so that the person leapt aside and dropped all his books and papers.

We did this again and again, never actually dousing anybody, but still laughing hysterically at the startled— and furious—reactions we produced. It was at least half an hour before Dad got to us. He didn't raise his voice; he just firmly told us to stop and made us mop up the muddy footprints on the floor. His red face was the only sign of emotion he displayed, and that was involuntary.

Often on summer weekends our family went on float trips on a beautiful, secluded river in the Ozarks. We had a canvas boat with a collapsible wooden frame, something like a kayak. After we unpacked upstream, a local garage mechanic would drive our car to a point far down the river and leave it parked there overnight.

We spent the next two days drifting down the river, pausing to swim in the clear water whenever we came to a good deep pool. Dad steered through the frequent rapids, shouting instructions at Mom, who would paddle frantically at the front of the boat. Sometimes Mom, who was not particularly skillful at this, maneuvered the boat into a rock, which would slash a hole in the canvas. Dad would curse briefly at Mom and then patiently dry and patch the boat.

When it began to get dark and the cicadas started their

gentle, scratchy song ("That noise makes the sun go down," Tycho once said), we stopped and camped at some nice woodsy place on the shore. Dad cooked steaks over an open fire, and Mom heated up canned baked beans, which always tasted delicious in the open air. We watched the stars come out and listened to the rushing water as we ate.

Once one of Dad's medical students and his wife came with us on a weekend camping trip at a spectacular swimming hole. You could swim down a series of small waterfalls, which led to a beautiful, deep pool surrounded by high granite cliffs, from which you could dive into the water.

The student's wife had brought fried chicken for Sunday lunch, wrapped in waxed paper in a wicker picnic basket. Everyone was enjoying the chicken, which was nicely crisp on the outside and moist within—until Dad, who ate slowly, smiled and held up a little white grub on his finger for us to see.

He had noticed it crawling around the interior of the drumstick he was eating. We all shrieked when we took a closer look at our own pieces of chicken and saw identical white grubs slithering around inside them, too. Enjoying our reaction, Dad explained that flies had easily made their way through the wicker and the loosely wrapped waxed paper to lay eggs inside the chicken the day before, and now the little larvae had hatched. He pointed out, amused, that they were *probably* harmless, nothing but protein. But the rest of us (even Vicky) felt sick and didn't eat another bite—which left more chicken for Dad to consume with his usual leisurely gusto.

On weekends when we didn't go to the country, Dad would sometimes entertain Vicky and me (when we were ten and under) by blindfolding us and driving us by a circuitous route to some point in the city that he knew was unfamiliar to us. We would then take off our blindfolds and get out of the car, and Dad would drive away, leaving us to find our own way home. He never worried, no matter how long it took us. He made sure we had one dime, so that we could call home if we were still lost when it got dark. Vicky and I had fun finding our way back together, feeling like Hansel and Gretel.

The only time we used the dime was when two of our friends came along. These kids got scared when we found no recognizable landmarks after several hours of wandering. Vicky and I weren't worried, but we let our friends use the dime to call *their* parents from a pay phone. Their parents were hysterical—and though we described our surroundings, they couldn't figure out where we were. We didn't have another dime. The parents told us not to move—and *not* to talk to strangers.

Then they called Dad, who had just started eating his lunch. "Where are they?" they furiously demanded.

"Beats me," Dad said. "I left them in that warehouse

district over on the other side of the highway—but that was a couple of hours ago."

"The warehouse district!" they gasped. "We're driving over there this instant—and you better start looking, too!"

"Sure," Dad said agreeably. "But I'd suggest that one of you stay at home so that—"

They hung up before listening to Dad's advice, called the police, and frantically set out to find us.

Dad went back to his lunch, meticulously peeling and slicing an apple, toasting pieces of cheese on buttered bread, sipping from a glass of red wine while reading the paper with his usual thoroughness. Then he got in the car and located us in ten minutes.

Our friends' parents had been too hysterical to listen to Dad's rational advice and had *both* rushed out to search for us, leaving no one at home to answer the phone. There was no way to tell them their kids were okay. They didn't get back for hours. The police went on looking for us the whole time as well; none of us knew the cops had been called, so no one informed them we had been found. After that, Vicky and I saw these friends only at *their* house.

In high school, when Vicky and I became the center of our circle of oddball friends, we always had a special celebration on the Fourth of July in honor of Vicky's birthday, which was actually July 15. Dozens of kids brought food for a potluck supper at our house. One reason this party was particularly festive was that we all sat and ate and drank at one tremendously long table in the backyard, which gave the event the feeling of a royal banquet. Dad helped us make this table out of the many old doors he collected and saved in the basement.

These parties were some of the few times we benefited from one of Dad's most extreme peculiarities: He never throws anything away. Our basement was jammed with burned-out light bulbs, used fan belts, dead batteries, and piles of decades-old magazines and newspapers that he refused to part with, no matter how much Mom complained. One entire room in the basement was taken up by fifty army surplus mine-detector kits—he had seen them advertised somewhere for a dollar apiece and quickly snapped up every one of them. I don't remember what the mine detectors themselves were like, but they were packed in sturdy wooden crates; Dad was sure he'd find a use for those crates someday.

But most of this stuff he kept forever and never used. The doors were one exception; another, even more notable, was the treasured melted telephone he discovered while poking around the ruins of a recently burned-down office building. The body of the phone and the dial were very warped and lopsided where the plastic had been softened by the heat. Dad liked it because it looked like something from a Salvador Dali painting.

When Danny was in college, he found the melted telephone and actually got it to work. Danny proudly displayed the cartoonlike phone on his desk when he was a scientist at Bell Laboratories, and he uses it to this day.

Another reason for Vicky's birthday celebrations being particularly festive was that Mom and Dad went out, leaving us and our friends to party without adult supervision. Most of the time, of course, it was an advantage not to be restricted by parents. But on Vicky's seventeenth birthday, it was *not* an advantage that no adults were around when the police showed up with a warrant for Vicky's arrest. The cops wouldn't explain what they were arresting her for. They just sternly flashed their badges and ID's; thrust legal documents at Vicky, whose long blonde hair was in its usual disarray; and actually snapped a pair of handcuffs on her.

"But you can't do this!" Vicky protested as they led her away. "It's my *birth*day party—and it's the Fourth of July!"

"Crime doesn't take a holiday," one of the cops grimly remarked.

Mom and Dad were at someone's cottage out in the country; we didn't have the phone number, and it took us quite a while to find it. By the time they got to the police station, Vicky had been there for several hours. The police had roughly strip-searched her and then locked her up in a cell, still refusing to tell her what her crime was supposed to be. Only when Mom and Dad arrived did they reveal that she had been arrested for writing hundreds of dollars' worth of bad checks.

Vicky was not the most obedient teenager, but writing bad checks was not in her repertoire. Mom was furious at the police.

"Shut up, darling," Dad said and calmly explained that Vicky had lost her wallet, with her driver's license in it, at a downtown movie theater several weeks before. She had already applied for a new license. In the meantime, someone who resembled Vicky's photo on the old license had obviously used it as an ID to pass bad checks in her name.

The cops didn't buy it.

"Shut up, darling," Dad told Mom again and called a friend who was a civil rights lawyer. He couldn't take the case, since it wasn't in his field, but he gave Dad the name of a criminal lawyer who knew what to do to get the police to release Vicky on bail. She would still have to undergo criminal proceedings.

As frightening as it had been for Vicky to be locked up without explanation, she made the most of it once she was released. She was the only person any of us knew who had been in jail, and everyone was terribly curious and impressed. Vicky did a hilarious impersonation of the matron who had searched her, right down to her drawl and her particularly disgusting way of chewing gum.

The criminal lawyer was not so amusing. He was a smooth type, who wore a jazzy suit and very expensive pointed shoes. Mom wanted to fire him during his first consultation with Vicky, when he told Vicky it was okay for her to admit to *him* that she had really written the checks. Dad pulled Mom out of the room and explained to her that criminal lawyers always asked questions like that. But Vicky was upset and worried when he left; she found it frustrating that he blandly refused to believe her repeated insistence that she was innocent.

Later, Dad told the lawyer in private that Vicky wouldn't have written bad checks—she just didn't think that way and, anyway, she was given money whenever she asked for it. The lawyer said that all middle-class teenagers were the same; they cared only about money and clothes and being just like everybody else. The lawyer knew Vicky had done it, but he would still take the case. Dad knew Vicky *hadn't* done it, but since this guy had been highly recommended to him by a trusted friend, he kept him on.

Dad also maintained control during the lineup. The store clerk who had accepted one of the bad checks was summoned to the police station to see if she could identify the criminal. Vicky stood on a sort of stage at the front of the room in a line with several other females chosen by the police from their secretarial staff. All the other women in the lineup were decades older than Vicky and had short, dark hair.

The clerk studied them for awhile, then murmured that Vicky was wearing earrings like the girl who had passed the check and declared that Vicky was the culprit.

"Shut up, darling," Dad said when Mom started to protest and then quietly pointed out the obvious to the lawyer, who explained it to the police. The girl who had passed the checks must have looked something like Vicky or else she couldn't have gotten away with using Vicky's license, with her photo on it, as an ID. Naturally the clerk had identified Vicky, who was the only blonde and the only teenager in the lineup.

Now Vicky and Mom were both tense and afraid, and therefore sullen and quarrelsome at home, eating little, snapping at each other more than usual. Dad did not let this distract him, losing himself in the paper, practicing the violin, relishing his food.

The lawyer told him it was really a tough case—he and the police both felt the clerk's identification of Vicky was very incriminating, despite the complete illogic of the lineup. Dad suggested a handwriting sample. "They have copies of the checks," he told the lawyer. "All we have to do is have the handwriting analyzed and prove it's not the same as Vicky's."

The lawyer, believing Vicky to be guilty, was against this. Dad insisted on getting a copy of one of the checks

from the DA's office and showing it to a police handwriting expert, along with an example of Vicky's handwriting. The expert stated unequivocally that Vicky could
not have written the checks. On that basis, she was declared innocent, her name cleared of any criminal record.

At the party afterward, now that she was vindicated,
Vicky felt free to add a scathing version of the lawyer to
her repertoire of characters. Mom pointed out to everyone
that the successful outcome was entirely the result of
Dad's shrewdness and clear thinking, in spite of the ob-
noxious lawyer, who had done nothing constructive and
probably *still* believed Vicky was guilty.

Some of our friends were a little afraid of Dad, mis-
interpreting his detached demeanor as critical, even
menacing. But his children all came to learn that we
could go to Dad with any problem—even the most hu-
miliating situations that had resulted from our own in-
eptitude or selfishness or gross bad judgment—and
instead of getting angry, he would try to come up with
the most efficient solution.

When I was a senior in high school, I was accepted at
Harvard, as an early admission, in January. This ac-
ceptance was not based on my grades—I was 87th in a
class of 530. What got me in was high scores on the
standardized SAT and National Merit tests and my many
creative extracurricular activities. Also, I had snowed the
Harvard dean of admissions, who had come to interview

people at our school in the fall—I told him I had gone to the Yale interview in order to get out of gym, which he found highly amusing. (I also told the Yale guy I went to the Harvard interview to get out of gym, but I don't know if that worked as well, since I didn't apply to Yale.) Of course, Mom was thrilled that I had been accepted by Harvard and told everyone. I was happy about it, too.

April 15 was the day that students were normally notified by colleges. ("April is the cruelest month," Matilda was fond of quoting.) I, like many others, was called to the office for a phone call on that day. I blithely assumed it was Mom, informing me that Harvard had granted me a scholarship. But Mom's voice on the phone was hoarse with misery. "They changed their minds and *rejected* you because of your grades," she moaned.

I was somewhat downcast by this and felt guilty about my grades but did not consider it a tragedy, since the University of Chicago had accepted me. But when I got home from school that day, Mom was in a woeful state; it was the only time in my life I ever saw her drinking at three-thirty in the afternoon. As truly unconventional as Mom is, as genuinely unconcerned with other peoples' opinions, she is not totally immune to certain forms of status, academic status in particular. She was a lot more unhappy about the rejection than I was.

Mom hadn't been able to reach Dad at work. When he got home that evening and Mom emotionally broke the tragic news to him, he responded with his usual distant, noncommittal "Huh" and sat down with the paper.

But eventually he made a few phone calls. He spoke to the dean of the medical school where he worked and other department heads at the university, several of them with Ph.D.s from Harvard and all of them widely recognized academics. They were more than willing to write letters to the Harvard dean of admissions, pointing out that his treatment of me was lacking in professional ethics. Mom wanted to write him, too. Dad advised her not to. Instead, he waited until his colleagues' letters had arrived in Cambridge and phoned the dean himself.

Dad was very polite, and calm and reasonable as always. He even managed to be jocular. In a pleasant, conversational voice, he pointed out that it was really not the best policy to unconditionally accept someone—influencing him to turn down offers from other schools—and then reject him without warning three months later. The Harvard dean could hardly dispute this impeccable logic, especially since Dad was not the least bit emotional or argumentative, as most other parents would have been.

It was almost certainly on the basis of Dad's cool behavior during this phone call that Harvard decided to accept me, after all—where I went on to spend the four most miserable years of my life.

Oddballs

I lied.

Writers of fiction always do. We take something from life and then tidy it up, tying loose ends together, changing the results of actions, arranging situations to suit our whims, playing God. We do this because it's fun—and to make our stories appear to *mean* something, which events rarely do in real life.

But—though it's possible that I may have exaggerated slightly in a few instances—I have told only one *real* lie about my family in this book. Except for that, everything I've described did happen, and that's the truth, whether the reader chooses to believe it or not. The single story in which I actually invented something is "The Hypnotist."

Don't get me wrong. Jack did hypnotize Tycho. Tycho really drank water out of the toilet and appeared to be under the influence of a post-hypnotic suggestion to throw the nearest object to the floor whenever he heard the word *window.* The only part I made up was the tidy little suggestion at the end that Jack used his hypnotic powers to make Danny stop picking on Tycho.

When Danny was around eleven or twelve, he did stop abusing Tycho, but it had nothing to do with hypnosis. The ostensible reason for this change was that Tycho suddenly grew taller and stronger than Danny and was now capable of beating him up.

But there was more to Danny's change than Tycho's size, since he knew that easygoing Tycho would rarely strike back. And for a while, he did go on flinging insults at him.

"*You* can't come to the movies with us, Tycho," Danny said one Saturday afternoon, as he and a friend were putting on their jackets.

Tycho, who was practicing the cello in the front hall, shrugged indifferently, not lifting his eyes from the music.

"Let's get out of here," Danny's friend said, putting his hands over his ears. "That horrible noise is driving me crazy."

"That's not noise! Tycho plays really good," Danny said, suddenly turning on his friend.

"Tycho was messing things up in my room," Danny complained to Mom a few days later. "He did something with my Phillips screwdriver, and now I can't find it."

"I've told you a million times to leave Danny's things alone, Tycho," Mom snapped at him. "Don't you ever listen?"

Tycho placidly turned a page of his book. "Danny left the Phillips screwdriver down in the basement yesterday," he said.

"Oh," Danny said, after a minute. "That's right, I did. You shouldn't get mad at Tycho for something he didn't do, Mom. It's not fair."

This shocking and totally unexpected streak of decency and justness that began to surface in Danny (where had it come from?) eventually made it impossible for him to go on tormenting Tycho. Another factor was that they turned out to have many interests in common.

Together they built a Van de Graaf generator in the basement. It was a large metal ball atop a four-foot-high cylinder. When you put your finger near the ball, a bright bolt of lightning would leap from the ball to the finger, spectacular in appearance but harmless and much less painful than you would have expected.

When Vicky and I had parties, we loved demonstrating it to our friends. We would all hold hands in the dark basement, and when one person put his hand near the ball, the fizzling arc of electricity looked just like something out of *The Bride of Frankenstein*. Everyone in the line could feel the startling but not very powerful electric jolt flowing through our bodies. Our friends thought Tycho and Danny were geniuses.

Danny is a computer scientist, Tycho a physicist. They both began their scientific careers at Bell Laboratories. A little joke of Danny's caused a sensation his first year there. The lab had an abundant supply of liquid nitrogen, a super-cold substance that boils at room temperature. Ingenious Danny poured some liquid nitrogen into an empty plastic soft-drink bottle, screwed the lid on tight, and left the bottle out in the corridor. In a few minutes the nitrogen boiled, and the expanding gas blew up the bottle. The tremendous explosion echoed up and down the long corridor, startling everybody on the floor. This act did little to increase Danny's popularity at work. But popularity has never been much of a motivating factor for any of us.

All four siblings are friends. Our personalities and styles of living have evolved differently, but in one respect the four of us are the same: We don't base our behavior on what other people will think about us.

Danny expresses his opinions bluntly, even when he knows other people may violently disagree with him—and they often do. He acts according to strict moral principles and can be quite unbending at times. He is also very outgoing and makes friends whenever he visits me. He has given me many creative ideas for my books.

Tycho has never owned a television; he would rather play the cello or go on four-day hikes in the mountains with his wife, Marina, a zoologist who has spent a lot of time studying primate behavior in the African jungle. They also lived in Zurich, Switzerland, for several years, where they had a beautiful house overlooking the lake, which was a ten-minute walk from the Lindt chocolate factory.

Vicky, a nurse, has not hesitated to tell *doctors* that they may have made a mistake about a patient. Her husband Dave—a true oddball to the core—did a lot of the child rearing while Vicky was at work. She and her daughter, Julie, who is as good an actress as Vicky, often participate in local theatrical productions—Julie won acclaim as one of the no-neck monsters in Tennessee Williams' *Cat on a Hot Tin Roof.* It was Julie who decided on her little brother's name, Spencer, well before he was born. Now she calls him Fluffy.

I have never had a full-time job in my life, though I worked part-time for many years as rehearsal pianist for a ballet company, touring with them all over Europe and the United States and having many memorable encounters with dancers and choreographers, some of them regrettably famous. But eventually the remorseless totalitarian regime of the ballet company began to make me feel a little sick. I hated working for an organization that treated everyone—dancers as well as staff—like dispensable plastic objects. I was also making enough money from writing to live on. So I quit. I currently live and write in Bangkok, Thailand—one of the hottest, ugliest, most polluted and congested cities in the world—because I am so happy here.

Most parents can't help loving their children, and I suspect that Mom and Dad might love us just as much even if we had—by some cruel and improbable joke of nature—turned out to be conventional. But it's a meaningless question.

Because, somehow or other, we have grown up to be the kind of oddballs that Mom and Dad like.